Home for Christmas

Books by Holly Chamberlin

LIVING SINGLE

THE SUMMER OF US

BABYLAND

BACK IN THE GAME

THE FRIENDS WE KEEP

TUSCAN HOLIDAY

ONE WEEK IN DECEMBER

THE FAMILY BEACH HOUSE

SUMMER FRIENDS

LAST SUMMER

THE SUMMER EVERYTHING CHANGED

THE BEACH QUILT

SUMMER WITH MY SISTERS

SEASHELL SEASON

THE SEASON OF US

HOME FOR THE SUMMER

HOME FOR CHRISTMAS

Published by Kensington Publishing Corporation

Home for
Christmas

Holly
Chamberlin

KENSINGTON BOOKS
http://www.kensingtonbooks.com

KENSINGTON BOOKS are published by

Kensington Publishing Corp.
119 West 40th Street
New York, NY 10018

All Kensington titles, imprints and distributed lines are available at special quantity discounts for bulk purchases for sales promotion, premiums, fund-raising, educational or institutional use.

Special book excerpts or customized printings can also be created to fit specific needs. For details, write or phone the office of the Kensington Special Sales Manager: Kensington Publishing Corp., 119 West 40th Street, New York, NY, 10018, Attn. Special Sales Department. Phone: 1-800-221-2647.

Library of Congress Card Catalogue Number: 2017944857

ISBN-13: 978-1-4967-0684-3
ISBN-10: 1-4967-0684-6
First Kensington Hardcover Edition: November 2017

eISBN-13: 978-1-4967-0686-7
eISBN-10: 1-4967-0686-2
First Kensington Electronic Edition: November 2017

10 9 8 7 6 5 4 3 2 1

Printed in the United States of America

As always, for Stephen
And this time also for Connie

Acknowledgments

I have said it before but it bears repeating. There would be no Holly Chamberlin without John Scognamiglio. Thank you, John. Also, this is in memory of my aunt, Ann V. Donner.

"Our hearts grow tender with childhood memories and love of kindred, and we are better for having, in spirit, become a child again at Christmas-time."
—Laura Ingalls Wilder

Chapter 1

It was the eleventh of December, a crisp winter day with not a cloud in the sky to threaten rain or snow. Nell King shivered as she came down the stairs from the second floor and into the living room. It was her habit to keep the heat low during the day when she and the girls were most often out. While the habit saved money, it did mean that from about the middle of November through the end of March Nell, Molly, and Felicity went around the house bundled to the teeth. At the moment Nell was wearing a plaid flannel shirt over a thermal t-shirt, lined jeans, and wool slipper socks. Her dark hair was piled into a messy updo and her face was free of makeup.

Not that she ever wore much makeup these days. There was no need for concealment or for disguise, not in Nell's world, and though once upon a time she had taken pleasure in preening and primping, since her divorce six years earlier the idea of dressing and making up held virtually no appeal. At least she hadn't taken to wearing her pajamas and slippers out of the house. The day that happened, Nell thought, she would have let the whole casual thing go too far and would need a stylist's intervention.

With a feeling of satisfaction Nell surveyed the living room. She had begun decorating for the Christmas season immediately after Thanksgiving. No sooner had the ears of Indian corn and the oddly shaped gourds and the sprays of red, orange, and yellow leaves been tucked away than the baubles and bows of Christmas made their appearance. The windows were outlined with tiny white lights. Fresh green garland was wound around the handrail of the stairs to the second floor. A large, cut-glass bowl was filled with colorful, glossy ribbon candy. A tall glass jar held an array of candy canes. Slabs of peanut brittle were artfully arranged on a rectangular ceramic plate with a pretty green glaze. A gingerbread house had pride of place on the coffee table. It was a full two feet high and sat on a base one foot square. The roof was comprised of round red-and-white peppermint candies. The window shutters were made of sticks of gum while the windowpanes had been crafted of leaf gelatin. Red M & Ms made up the house's two chimneys, and candy canes represented lampposts. Every surface that could be was heavily covered with colored fondant and marzipan.

But the real star of the holiday season was the massive evergreen tree waiting to be decorated with ornaments that held a special meaning for Nell and her daughters. There was the set of tiny angels dressed in Victorian garb that Nell's maternal grandmother had given her shortly before she died. There were the five crystal icicles Molly had won in a raffle back in middle school. And there was the figurine of Dr. Seuss's infamous Grinch that Felicity had bought with the money she had earned from her first paying job as a delivery person for the *Yorktide Daily Chronicle*.

Seventeen-year-old Felicity's eyes had popped when she

first saw this year's tree, its long branches gracefully spreading from its sturdy trunk. "This is the biggest tree we've ever had," she had said. "How did you get it through the front door?"

Nell had smiled enigmatically; in fact she had hired two young workers at the Christmas tree lot to deliver the tree and wrangle it into its stand, a new one Nell had purchased as the one she already owned was far too small for the trunk of this giant.

But one Christmas tree wasn't enough, not this year. A small artificial tree stood on a table on the landing of the second floor; it was hung with skeletons of starfish; seashells of various shapes and sizes; bits of green and blue sea glass; plastic lobsters; little wooden lobster traps; and a selection of ceramic moose, loons, puffins and bears.

"Uh, Mom," twenty-one-year-old Molly had said when Nell had been putting the final touches on the tree. "We know we live in Maine. We know we might run across a moose on the road at any time, though I seriously hope we don't."

"What's your point?" Nell had asked.

"It's just that a tree like this should be in the lobby of a hotel or a retail store. It's like an advertisement."

Nell's disappointment must have shown on her face because Molly had immediately added: "Sorry, Mom. I wasn't criticizing, really."

Another small tree stood on a sideboard in the dining room, this one decorated with ornaments related to Santa Claus in his various guises, from the stately and solemn St. Nicholas, secret gift-giver and patron saint of sailors; to the uniquely English versions of Father Christmas, clutching wassail bowls and dressed in furred and hooded gowns, with wreaths of holly encircling their heads; to the jolly, bearded American Santa of *Rudolph the Red-Nosed Reindeer* fame, with red suit trimmed in white fur, black boots and belt, and a hat tipped with a white fur pom-pom. This was the Santa Claus to be found in every mall in the United States from just after Thanksgiving until Christmas Eve, the Santa Claus who posed for pictures with small, often bewildered children perched on his lap. It was a matter of regret for Nell that she had never managed to get such a portrait of the girls with Santa. It hadn't been for lack of trying. Sheer bad luck had gotten in the way.

Nell had decorated the girls' bedrooms for the holidays, too, though with more restraint than she had employed with the rest of the house; she respected their rooms as private spaces, so she had confined herself to hanging a jingle bell from each doorknob and a fabric wall hanging on the back of each closet door.

As for Nell's own bedroom, well, it was empty of anything relating to Christmas other than the materials for the secret craft projects on which she was working. It simply hadn't seemed worth the effort to add a jingle bell or a wall hanging for her own enjoyment. And her daughters wouldn't notice; it had been years since either girl had come to her mother's room to cuddle with her in the new bed Nell had bought when they first moved to Yorktide. Her old bed, the one she had shared for more than fifteen years with Joel, had swiftly gone to a charity shop. Nell did not hate her ex-husband in spite of the fact that he had left her for his mistress, but neither did she need so solid a reminder of their past intimate life in her new home.

Nell continued on to the kitchen now, where the large square table was set up for the day's craft project. She took a seat, and as she did so she was suddenly overwhelmed by a sense of sadness tinged with bittersweet nostalgia. It wasn't the first time this season she had been overcome with these feelings, and she knew it would not be the last, for this Christmas might very well be the final one she would spend with both of her children under one roof. By this time the following year Nell thought it was likely that Molly would be married or at least engaged to Mick Williams, her longtime boyfriend, and as for Felicity . . .

The news had come as a very great shock. Felicity had spent the weekend after Thanksgiving in Boston with her father and stepmother and Pam's eight-year-old son, Taylor. On Sunday evening Nell met Felicity at the bus station at the old Pease Air Force Base off the turnpike in Portsmouth, and no sooner had Felicity slid into the passenger seat of Nell's serviceable Subaru than she had dropped her bombshell. "Dad and Pam have invited me to join them in Switzerland next Christmas! We'll be staying at a swanky ski lodge, and they're paying for everything, including my airfare. Isn't that fantastic? I can't wait for next year. I am *so* excited."

Nell had started the engine and steered the car out of the station. "Didn't you think to check with me first?" she asked as casually as she could manage, which wasn't very casually at all. Her heart was hurting.

"No," Felicity had replied promptly. "Why? Anyway, I am *so* looking forward to next year!"

"What about *this* Christmas?" Nell had asked, ignoring her daughter's unconsciously callous reply. "Aren't you looking forward to this Christmas with your sister and me at home in Maine?"

Felicity had shrugged. "Yeah. But Europe, Mom! That's so much cooler. Who knows what sort of interesting people I might meet? Maybe even some gorgeous Italian guys. Let's face it, I know just about everybody in Yorktide by name and absolutely *everybody* by sight. Nothing new or exciting ever happens here. Boring!"

Well, Nell supposed Yorktide would seem boring to a young woman of Felicity's vibrant and outgoing personality. Still, Felicity had never expressed boredom with her home before, not until her stepmother had filled her head with visions of exotic places peopled by immoral millionaires and overrated actors and who knew what other dubious types!

Nell took a deep and calming breath, picked up the container of Elmer's glue, and attempted to concentrate on the task at hand. It was not easy to do. Since Felicity's momentous announcement Nell had been fixated on the fact that both of her children would soon be leaving home, and the idea filled her with dread. Next August Felicity would be a freshman at the University of Michigan in Ann Arbor. And while it was true that Molly would still be local after her marriage to Mick, whenever exactly that took place, she would have her own life to live, a husband and in-laws and, sooner rather than later, children for whom to care. Add to that the duties demanded of Molly as a farmer's wife, including her continuing involvement with the Maine Farm Bureau, where Mick was a member of the Young Farmer and Rancher Committee, and there was little doubt in Nell's mind that even at the best of times she would see her older daughter only once or twice a week.

The house on Trinity Lane, the cozy and charming house in which Nell and her daughters had lived happily for the past six years, would feel horribly empty before long. It had been a risk to relocate the girls from Drayton, Massachusetts, to Yorktide, where they knew absolutely no one, but it had been important to Nell to remove her children from their stepmother's immediate influence. Pam Bertrand-King, Olympic gold medalist in skiing, often featured in the pages of the glossy magazines Felicity enjoyed, the face of high-end car companies and manufacturers of athletic clothing and trendy new jewelry designers. Molly and Felicity had indeed been upset about leaving old friends, but soon enough they had made new friends and found a warm welcome in southern Maine.

All three of the King women had fallen immediately in love with the classic white clapboard farmhouse, and Nell had set about decorating it to reflect *her* personality rather than her mother's. It was Jacqueline Emerson who had dictated the decorating of the house her daughter and son-in-law had moved into twenty-some-odd years earlier. Here, structured sofas had been replaced with comfy couches. Hard edges and clean lines had been left behind in favor of rounded corners and curves. A neutral palette of taupe, tan, and black had been rejected in favor of warm and vibrant pinks, reds, and greens. Flowers fresh from the garden arranged naturally in a milk jug had taken the place of a formal arrangement purchased weekly from a select florist. This house in Yorktide felt to Nell so much more *livable* than had the house back in Drayton.

Suddenly, Nell heard the front door open, followed by Felicity's distinctive lilting laugh and Molly's more subdued, serious tone. A moment or two later the girls came into the kitchen.

Molly was tall and athletically built, much like her father, something that had upset her for about a minute when at the age of twelve she was larger than most of her classmates. She had endured some teasing from boys and girls alike, but she had come through the difficult experience beautifully. That was Molly. She was never shaken for long. This afternoon she was wearing her favorite pair of eyeglasses, square, dark tortoiseshell frames.

Unlike her sister, Felicity was petite. Her long, dark brown hair was pulled into a high ponytail, a ponytail that tended to swing wildly when she strode through a room or bounded up a flight of stairs. Both girls were dressed in ubiquitous cold weather gear—puffer coats, lined leggings, boots from L. L. Bean, and super long wool scarves wound several times around their necks.

"Hey, Mom," Felicity said, giving her mother a kiss on the cheek. "What's all this?"

Nell smiled. "I'm making toy soldiers and snowmen."

"Since when have you been so into crafts?" Molly asked. "You've been working away at some project or another every day for weeks."

"I've always liked doing crafts," Nell protested.

"No you haven't," Molly countered, "except for the time you took that pottery class."

Felicity laughed. "No offense, Mom, but that jug you made was pretty awful. It didn't pour right and the color was really icky."

Nell shrugged. "Pottery just wasn't my thing."

"And making toy soldiers out of gum drops and snowmen out of marshmallows is your thing?" Molly asked, taking a green gumdrop from the pile on the table and popping it into her mouth.

"You have to admit it's a cute idea," Nell protested. "I found it in a Christmas craft book I got at the library."

"But what are we supposed to *do* with them?" Molly asked.

"Well, you anchor the supporting stick of each figure into a white Styrofoam block and then you have a row of soldiers and snowmen standing in the snow," Nell explained. "The Styrofoam represents the snow."

Molly raised an eyebrow. "If you say so." Her cell phone rang; she pulled it from her pocket and frowned at the screen.

"Who is it?" Nell asked.

"Mick. I'll call him back later."

For a brief moment Nell wondered why Molly had frowned. Maybe Molly had had a spat with Mick, though Mick was so good-natured Nell found it hard to imagine anyone being out of sorts with him for long. Mick had graduated college two years earlier with a degree in agricultural studies and had sound plans for expanding his family's farm. A young woman could do an awful lot worse than to marry Mick Williams.

"Do you want me to handle dinner, Mom?" Molly asked. "I could make hamburgers."

"That's okay," Nell replied. "I've got dinner planned."

"Then I'm going to take a hot shower," Molly announced. "I can't seem to shake this chill I got when I stopped to help Mr. Milton change a tire."

"And I need to start my math homework," Felicity added. "I hate trigonometry. I don't know why I have to take it when there's no way I'm going to ever use it."

When both girls had gone upstairs and Nell was sitting alone in the midst of half-constructed candy soldiers and marshmallow snowmen, she felt that too familiar wave of sadness wash over her again. She thought about the pinecones she had covered in silver-and-gold glitter; the fat pillar candles around which she had wrapped bright red ribbon; the tree-shaped napkin rings she had made out of construction paper; the place cards in the shape of holly leaves; the red and white poinsettia plants she had arranged in groups around the house. Christmas crafts, no matter how beautiful or charming, weren't going to stop the inevitable from happening. Nell knew that. And yet she continued to squeeze glue and sprinkle glitter and wield knitting needles in some vain and vaguely superstitious attempt to keep her children where they belonged. At home with their mother.

Chapter 2

While Molly set the table with the Kings' plain white plates, Felicity poured water into three tall everyday glasses. Nell rarely used the Waterford crystal and the Lenox tableware she had received at her wedding shower. The pieces held too many memories of the days when Nell and Joel King had been—or at least had appeared to be—a happy couple.

"That smells soooo good," Felicity said, refilling the pitcher at the sink.

Nell smiled. "I know." She had made batch upon batch of pesto during the summer, harvesting the basil from the garden, until the freezer was full of containers that brought back memories of the days when the sun provided light if not warmth until eight or nine o'clock.

"What did Mick want earlier?" Nell asked as the three took their seats around the table and began to eat.

"Nothing," Molly said.

"It couldn't really have been nothing," Felicity pointed out. "There has to be some intention behind calling some-one, even if it's just to say hi."

"Okay, he called to say hi."

"See?" Felicity cleared her throat and looked meaningfully at her mother. "I was looking again online at the J. W. Anderson bag I really want for Christmas. It's made in Spain."

"I know," Nell said. "You already told me."

"So what if it's made in Spain?" Molly asked.

"It means the workmanship is high quality. A bag like that is an investment piece."

Molly laughed. "What does a seventeen-year-old need with an investment piece? And it's not even something important. It's just a *bag*."

"Women keep their designer bags forever," Felicity argued. "One day I could pass it on to my own daughter."

"Assuming it hasn't gotten lost or stolen or hasn't totally fallen apart."

While her daughters argued about the relative importance of a handbag, Nell thought about the larger issue at hand. Before Felicity had announced her plans to spend next Christmas with her father and stepmother, Nell had considered the coveted bag out of the question. Since her daughter's announcement, however, she had given the idea of buying the bag serious consideration. If Pam and Joel could give Felicity a trip to Europe, the least Nell could do was to give her something equally extravagant. She might be able to scrape together the money, even though her salary as office manager of Mutts and Meows, a local veterinary practice, wasn't grand. And there were online luxury consignment stores, though the chances of a new design having already been given up for sale seemed low.

Nell suddenly became aware that her daughters' friendly disagreement was threatening to turn into an outright argument about the dangers of materialism. "I was reading an article in today's *Portland Press Herald*," she interrupted. "It was about the Yorktide and Oceanside Land

Bank Commission. Seems there are always volunteer posts open on the Emergency Shelter Assessment Committee."

"That's the bunch of services and government reps and advocates who make sure the homeless are safe and taken care of?" Felicity asked, using tongs to add more pasta to her plate.

"Right. I was thinking that once Molly graduates next June she'll have some time to give back to the community." Nell turned to her older daughter. "I thought you might be interested since you took that advanced psychology seminar last year on the causes of homelessness and what being homeless does to a person's state of mind."

"Some of the stuff you told us really freaked me out," Felicity said to her sister. "Like that when a non-homeless person looks at a homeless person, the part of the brain that activates when relating to other people and empathizing with them *fails* to activate."

"The medial prefrontal cortex," Molly said without looking up from her plate.

"It's like the brain dehumanizes the homeless before, I don't know, before a person can really see an *individual*." Felicity shuddered. "Awful."

"It is awful," Nell agreed. "This article said that last month on any given night there were an average of four hundred and thirty people in shelters in Portland alone. That's an appalling number."

"Molly *could* volunteer," Felicity said, "if co-managing the Williams's farm doesn't kill her! Farmers don't exactly have a lot of downtime."

"Molly won't be co-managing the farm until she and Mick are married," Nell pointed out. "Before that she'll have some room in her schedule."

Molly didn't comment.

"This pasta is awesome," Felicity said, heaping yet more onto her plate.

Clearly, Nell thought, her daughters were done with the subject of volunteering. "Do you taste the special ingredient in the salad dressing?" she asked. "It's coriander."

Felicity shrugged. "I can never identify individual ingredients. Frankly, as long as there's a lot of something, I'll probably enjoy it."

For a moment Nell wondered if Pam was a good cook, but it wasn't a question she would ask Felicity. She didn't need to know that Pam was as proficient in the kitchen as she was at so many other things. Like winning gold medals and luring other people's children to Switzerland for Christmas.

Molly suddenly got up from her seat and brought her plate and glass to the sink. "I've got some homework to do," she said.

"Can I help you clean up, Mom?" Felicity asked. "I know teenagers aren't supposed to complain about their mothers doing their chores, but seriously, you didn't have to vacuum my room and do my laundry yesterday. Those are my jobs, even though I'm not very good at them."

"That's okay. Cleaning up is exercise, right? All the bending and reaching. And I'm sure you have homework, too, like that trig you mentioned before dinner."

"Ugh," Felicity said. "I still have three more problems to solve."

When both girls had gone upstairs, Nell looked at the dirty plates and empty glasses with a sort of fondness. Some day in the not too distant future she would be making meals for one and cleaning up after only herself. She felt a keen wave of loneliness come over her and considered calling her closest friend and neighbor Jill for no other reason than to hear her voice. Nell had pulled her cell phone from her pocket before she decided not to make the call. *I'd better get used to being on my own,* she thought, striding toward the dishwasher with her own plate and glass. *I'd better get used to the sound of my own thoughts.*

Chapter 3

The house seemed oddly quiet until Nell remembered that Felicity had left for school at six-thirty that morning. When Felicity was in the house you knew it. Molly, who didn't have a class until nine, was probably somewhere about, but she was generally quiet and careful in her movements, not likely to be charging up and down the stairs, dropping cups on the kitchen floor, or accidentally letting doors slam behind her.

Nell sat on the edge of her bed, surrounded by books and magazines dedicated to holiday crafts. In a shopping bag on the floor were several skeins of wool, knitting needles, and the half-completed Christmas stockings she was determined to finish by Christmas Eve. Nell hated knitting and was remarkably bad at it, and true, the girls already had stockings their paternal grandmother had given them long ago, but as part of her plan to give her daughters a Christmas they would never forget, Nell was forging ahead with this project.

Other projects were more successful. One of the craft books Nell had borrowed from the library suggested wrapping one's Christmas gifts in plain brown paper decorated with images cut from old Christmas cards and magazines. The process of arranging the images to create a pleasing effect was time consuming and Nell wasn't at all sure the girls would appreciate her efforts. Still, she continued to paste images of Santa's reindeers, of angels in long white robes, and of Christmas wreaths decorated with red and green lights onto sheets of plain brown paper with a will.

The coveted J. W. Anderson bag aside, Nell had already purchased a few gifts for the girls: colorful wool socks for both, a new nightgown for Molly, a pair of fingerless gloves for Felicity. In addition she had decided to give each girl one special heirloom. For Felicity, who loved jewelry, it was a white gold and diamond cocktail ring that had once belonged to Nell's great aunt Prudence Emerson. Nell hadn't worn it since the divorce, and it seemed a shame the ring be kept stowed away when it could be enjoyed. For Molly, who had been collecting napkin rings and candlesticks for years in anticipation of having her own home one day, it was a large Mikasa serving platter dating from the 1950s. That, too, had once belonged to Great Aunt Prudence, and Molly had loved it since she was a little girl.

Nell glanced at the digital clock on her bedside table and realized she had better get a move on if she was to be on time for work. She hurriedly stashed her craft materials back into the closet and headed downstairs to the kitchen. As was her habit, she first looked to the Advent calendar that hung on the wall by the fridge. It depicted a large Victorian style house with one window for every day of the month of December through the twenty-fourth. On the front door of the house was the number twenty-five. The image was sprinkled with white glitter to represent snow, and several carolers in Victorian dress stood at the far left of the image, their mouths open in song. Nell saw that

Felicity had already opened the window marked December twelfth.

"Morning."

Nell turned to see Molly standing in the doorway. "Good morning to you," she said. "I'll get the kettle going."

"Mom," Molly said. "I need to talk to you about something."

"Sure," Nell said, taking a seat at the table. "Join me. Coffee will be ready in a few minutes."

"I'd rather stand." Molly straightened her shoulders and tilted her head back a bit, as if she were about to deliver an oration. "I've given it a lot of thought, and I've decided to move to Boston after graduation in June."

"What do you mean?" Nell asked.

"I mean that I've always wanted to experience urban life."

"I don't understand," Nell said with a bit of a laugh. "Whenever we visit Boston you can't wait to get home. And the last time we were in New York the noise of the traffic drove you mad. You and Mick have both said that people who choose to live in a big city are crazy."

"Well, things have changed," Molly stated. "I want to meet new people and see new things. I feel stifled here. I'm beyond bored."

Nell stared up at her daughter; there was a look of set determination on her face, and suddenly Nell recalled what Felicity had said when she came home from her last trip to Boston. She, too, had said that life here in Yorktide was boring. Did her daughters really mean that life with their mother was boring? And where was Mick in all this? Had Molly suddenly broken up with him? *Don't jump to conclusions,* Nell told herself. *Listen to what Molly has to say.*

"So," she asked, "are you saying that you need a sort of vacation?"

"I'm saying," Molly replied, "that I want to *do* something important before it's too late. I want to focus on achieving something."

Nell felt her head swim. She had so many questions. For one, what did Molly mean by "too late"? For another, wasn't managing a thriving farm with the person you loved doing something important?

"Molly," she said. "Please sit."

Molly did, though with an air of reluctance.

"Have you made any firm plans?" Nell asked, careful to keep her tone neutral.

Molly placed her hands flat on the table. "No," she said.

"Have you started looking for a job?" Nell asked. "Have you thought about what sort of work you'll be qualified for?"

Molly drew her hands off the table and onto her lap. "No. There's time for all that. I'll set up interviews during spring break. And I'll start the hunt for an apartment then, too."

Nell took a deep breath and decided to ask a different sort of question. "Has anything happened to make you unhappy here?" she asked. "Has Mick done anything wrong? Have you two had a falling out? Have I said something to hurt you?"

Molly sighed. "No," she said. "Mick and I haven't had a falling out and no one said or did anything wrong. It's just that I've realized there's so much *else* out there. That's why I didn't say anything when at dinner last night you were talking about volunteering. I'm not going to be around to give back to Yorktide. I want to experience the world before settling down to marriage and kids. Assuming I ever *do* settle down. I mean, I know I've *talked* about getting married and having a family, but I've changed my mind about all that."

Ah, Nell thought with a sinking heart. *"Too late" means marriage and children.* She wondered what sort of example she had set her daughters, forgoing a career to marry right out of college. Maybe it hadn't been a very good example. "What does Mick have to say about all this?" she asked. "You've done more than just *talk* with him about marrying and starting a family. You've *promised* him it's what you want. You've promised each other."

Molly looked into the middle distance. When she spoke, her tone was oddly cold. "It doesn't matter what Mick has to say or what I've said in the past. I'm going to end things with him after Christmas."

Nell felt as if she had been dealt a physical blow. "I don't understand," she said, hearing the rising note of distress in her voice. "You love Mick. You're going to be married. We've talked about what kind of dress you're going to wear and what you're going to serve at the reception. We've talked about the flowers and the favors. And after the wedding you and Mick are going to manage the farm together and someday you'll own it outright and pass it on to your children when they come of age. It's the life you've always wanted."

"It's the life I *thought* I wanted." Molly looked back to her mother, and the expression in her eyes was more than determined. It was hard. Nell had never before seen that look on her daughter's face. "Look, Mom," Molly went on. "Mick's been the only guy in my life. I can't just marry him and never know what it's like to be with another man. No one does that anymore. It's old-fashioned. It's ridiculous."

"But . . ."

"But what?" Molly said fiercely. "Look, I'm moving away from here and you know that Mick won't ever walk away from the farm. It's an impossible situation, Mom."

Nell put her hand to her forehead. "Have you told him how you feel?" she asked.

"No. I haven't told him anything."

Nell leaned forward in her chair. "Molly, please help me to understand. Are you saying that if Mick agreed to leave the farm and move with you to Boston you'd be happy?"

Molly rose abruptly from her seat. "Yes. No. Look, I'm not changing my mind so don't ask me to."

Nell felt sick. She was all too clearly reminded of how when she was Molly's age she had left the man she truly loved for someone her parents had convinced her was the better, more sensible choice as a husband. The truth was that no one was capable of making smart decisions at the tender age of twenty-one and they shouldn't even try, not without first consulting someone older and wiser, someone who had made plenty of mistakes they had lived to regret. Someone who was mature enough to admit her mistakes and to own up to the regrets. Before Nell could open her mouth to say something to that effect, Molly spoke again.

"I haven't told Fliss that I'm going to break up with Mick after the holidays. You know how she feels about him. She considers him a brother. So don't say anything to her, okay?"

Nell nodded. "All right," she said, her voice catching.

"Last night I told her that after graduation I'm probably going to get an apartment in Boston with some girls for a few months. That's all she needs to know for now. And don't tell Jill either about my breaking up with Mick, okay?"

Nell nodded again but said nothing.

"I'm going to be late for psych lab. I'll see you later, Mom."

Molly left the kitchen. Nell remained seated at the table

and attempted to process what she had just heard. Molly's decision to radically alter the plans she had set for her life seemed to have come from out of the blue, but the decision had to have a source. If only Nell could discover that source. Molly had been so *sure* about wanting to marry Mick and have a family with him. And Nell had relied on that scenario. It would have given her a continuing role in the life of her older daughter. *Molly was planning my future for me,* Nell realized. *I allowed her to promise me a life. But now . . .*

The furious whistling of the kettle startled Nell into action. She looked at the wall clock above the microwave. She had just enough time to grab a cup of coffee before leaving for work. Suddenly, she couldn't wait to be in the company of her cheerful colleagues at Mutts and Meows.

Chapter 4

"I binge watched the first season of *The Crown* again yesterday." Jill shook her head. "What did we ever do before Netflix and Acorn and Hulu?"

Nell dumped a measure of flour into the food processor and smiled. "We read a lot more."

Jill Smith, Nell's neighbor and closest friend in Yorktide, was a youthful seventy years old. Her hair was thick and silvery and she wore it in a sharp bob. Jill had an impressive collection of jewelry set with all sorts of stones, from pyrite to malachite, from jasper to peridot, from rough diamonds to rutilated quartz. This morning she was wearing a suite of turquoise stones set in yellow gold. The bright blue of the stone complemented the bright blue of her eyes.

"Nothing against books," Jill said, "but TV really is pretty fantastic these days."

Nell added a bit of water to the mixture she was concocting. "You're a television addict, Jill," she said.

Jill shrugged. "I'm retired. I'm allowed to vegetate."

"You'll never vegetate," Nell remarked. "You'll be surprising us all until the very end, and I hope that end is a long way away."

"Sheesh," Jill said. "Me too. I've survived too many rough times to chuck it all in now."

Life had indeed challenged Jill Smith, Nell reflected. When some forty-odd years earlier she found out she was pregnant, the father of her child demanded she have an abortion. When Jill refused, the cad hit the road, leaving her to raise her son on her own while building a successful gardening business. Jill had sold the business a few years back but still occasionally consulted for the new owners, had many friends, and was a docent at no fewer than three historical sites in Maine and New Hampshire.

But retirement wasn't all rosy. Jill's long-time beau had died the previous summer after a brief illness. Nell still had trouble accepting the fact that Brian Speer, a veritable force of nature, was gone from their lives. Brian, a retired banker, had been widowed when his son, Charlie, was only six and had raised the boy on his own. Charlie, now in his forties, had considered his father his dearest friend and had taken to Jill from the start. Jill's son, Stuart, not the most predictable fellow, had nevertheless taken to Brian. How Jill managed to bear her loss without falling to pieces was anyone's guess.

"What's in the oven?" Jill asked, interrupting Nell's musings.

"Blondies. I found a recipe that calls for the addition of coconut flakes and I thought it sounded interesting."

"Never a big fan of coconut," Jill said. "But if you've got any of those marzipan thingies left, I'll have one of those."

There were indeed still a few marzipan fruit-shaped candies left over from the other day's candy making, and Nell fetched the tin. "I've got some very upsetting news to share," she said, handing the tin to Jill.

Jill took a bite of a candy. "I'm listening. Yum. I love almond."

So Nell told her what Molly had announced earlier. "She contradicted herself," she said at the end of her tale. "On the one hand she said she wants to be with other men. On the other, she implied that the reason she's breaking up with Mick is because he won't leave Maine."

"Sounds like she doesn't really know what she wants. Not uncommon at her age. I read somewhere that it takes the human brain twenty-five years to fully mature."

Nell shook her head. "I had visions of being one of the grandmas down the road. I just assumed that Molly's life was going to play out the way she said it would and that my own life would follow right alongside."

Jill raised an eyebrow. "You know what they say about assuming?"

"Yes, I do. It's foolish. But Molly seemed to be *promising* she would stay here in Maine."

"Promising who?" Jill challenged. "Not you, Nell. Maybe Mick and maybe even herself, but not her mother."

"I know but . . ." Nell sighed. "I always expected that Felicity would fly far from the nest one day. But not Molly. She's always been so rooted and content. You know, I was planning to give her my great aunt Prudence's favorite serving platter for Christmas. Now I'm not so sure Molly would appreciate the platter, not since she's turned her back on getting married and starting a family."

"Single women need platters, too, Nell," Jill pointed out. "They give dinner parties just like married women."

"I know. I'm being silly. It's just that I pictured going to Mick and Molly's house on Sundays for dinner and Molly using the platter to serve the roast chicken and my helping to clean up afterwards and . . ."

"And all of you living happily ever after?" Jill sighed. "Sounds like you've got a major case of empty nest syndrome, Nell. Even the rooted ones move on. At least, they should."

"Were you devastated when Stuart left home?" Nell asked.

"Not devastated, no," Jill explained, "but not entirely happy, either. It was just the two of us for so long. Look, have you considered reaching out for some advice on how to handle the girls fleeing the coop?"

"No," Nell admitted. "I haven't, but it's probably a wise idea."

"Good," Jill said, reaching for the woolly scarf she had tossed onto the counter upon her arrival. "Then I'll leave you to your blondies. Um, could I have another marzipan thingie for the road?"

"Take the tin. I'll make more. And by the way, what I told you is top secret. Molly doesn't want anyone to know yet, not even Felicity, but I really needed to talk."

Jill smiled. "My mouth will be too full of candy to say a word."

Chapter 5

Molly had gone to Mick's parents' house for dinner, a weekly occurrence since the very earliest days of their relationship. Nell had sat at her own table with Felicity, trying to imagine what was going on around the Williamses' table that evening. She wondered if Mick had detected signs of Molly's withdrawing from him. He might not have, because he was extremely busy with running the farm. And why would he think that his girlfriend of almost six years was about to run off? If he did detect some unusual moods, he might simply attribute them to the difficult emotions a holiday could stir up. Mick was well aware of Molly's troubled relationship with her father. He might assume that memories of the Christmases before the divorce were plaguing the woman who was effectively his fiancée.

While Nell's thoughts had been with Molly, Felicity had gone on about how Pam had emailed her to say that she had gotten another promotional deal, this time with a big watch company Nell had never even heard of, and that the company was flying her to Los Angeles for the first photo shoot and that if Felicity wanted, she could have Pam's Rolex because as part of the deal she had signed with this premier company Pam would be given their latest model ladies' watch and would be expected to wear it in public. Nell had given the trusty Fossil watch she had been wearing every day for the past four years a surreptitious look and pretended to be interested in Pam's news.

Now in her room, the kitchen tidied and Felicity doing her homework, Nell reached for her cell phone. She didn't like to turn to her ex-husband for advice and certainly not for comfort, but when it came to their children she put her own feelings aside. Still, she hoped that Pam wouldn't answer the phone. Nell didn't feel up to hearing that perky voice that announced by its very tone that the speaker was beautiful and successful and a good deal younger than her husband's ex-wife. Little wonder Joel had fallen for Pam hook, line, and sinker when they met at a very expensive fund-raising dinner for a very fashionable cause that Nell had been too sick with the flu to attend.

Fortunately, Joel answered.

"I hope I'm not interrupting anything important," Nell began, sitting back against the pillows on her bed.

"No. Taylor's asleep and Pam just headed out to meet some friends. What's up? Are the girls okay?"

So Nell told him about Molly's decision to end her relationship with Mick and to move to Boston with, it seemed, no particular plan in place. "It's come out of the blue," Nell told him. "I can't understand it at all."

"Maybe she just has cold feet," Joel suggested. "Maybe she just needs to sow a few wild oats before settling down."

"But she's never been the cowardly or the wild type," Nell protested.

"Well," Joel said, "whatever her motive, I'll be happy to help support her until she finds a decent job. And I'm sure Pam won't mind if she wants to stay at our apartment.

We're hardly ever there." Joel sighed. "But why do I think she'll reject my help? There's been no change in her attitude toward me, has there?"

"Sadly, no," Nell told him. "She doesn't talk much about it, but it's clear she's still angry about the divorce."

"Not about the divorce," Joel corrected. "About my instigating it."

"Things could change. Maybe when . . ." Nell laughed ruefully. "I was going to say that maybe when she has children of her own she'll feel moved enough to accept you back into her life. But now it looks as if she might not be having children any time soon, if ever."

"Don't leap to conclusions, Nell. You'll only drive yourself crazy."

But isn't that a mother's job? Nell asked silently. *To drive herself crazy?* "I'll try," she said. "Good night, Joel. Thanks for listening."

"Good night, Nell," he said. "Be well."

Nell plugged her cell phone into its charger, slipped into her favorite flannel nightgown, and brought her laptop into the bed. *Okay,* she thought. *Let's see what the experts have to say about empty nest syndrome.*

It didn't take long for Nell to realize that the experts had an awful lot to say. One website claimed that the transition from full-time mother to "independent woman" could take up to two years. *That was an interesting choice of words,* Nell thought. Were the authors of the website implying that a woman caring for young children was somehow dependent on those children as they were dependent on her? Another website advised that a mother be gentle with herself while grieving the loss of her children's presence under her roof. *Good advice,* Nell thought. If only she knew exactly what being gentle with one's self meant. A third site declared that sympathy for the grieving parent could be scarce as children leaving the nest was normal and indeed desirable. That was understandable. And yet another explained that making empty nest syndrome more difficult to bear for so many women was the fact that they were also going through menopause and that in addition many had the financial burden of helping to support their parents. Nell was not menopausal; neither was she funding her well-off parents. In fact, her parents didn't seem to need anything at all from her. Nor did her ex-husband. And soon, her daughters wouldn't need her, either. What then? "I'll have been made redundant," Nell whispered to the room. "Unnecessary. Unwanted." And who were you if you couldn't define yourself as someone who was *needed*?

Nell read on. This particular website urged that a person choose to see the "empty nest" as an opportunity to revive old interests. *But I have no interests other than my children,* Nell thought. And she hadn't had any other interests since the days when she had known and loved Eric Manville. *The* Eric Manville. Long before he had become a household name he had been her friend, her lover, and the greatest supporter of her passionate love for poetry. The man she had wanted to marry.

But that was all in the past. With a determined shake of her head, Nell exited the website and went on to another. The authors of this online support group opined that anticipation of the loss of a child under one's roof was often greater than the reality of the loss. They suggested a parent try to imagine particular moments without the child in the house, for example, a Saturday evening or a Monday morning. "Without X, there is Y," was the structure of this imaginative exercise. The future, referred to on this site as the "post-parental period," should be seen as a time of great freedom. Post-parental. Nell shuddered. It was a cold and awful term.

Nell had had enough. She shut the laptop, turned out the light on her bedside table, and slid under the covers. She had taken her friend's suggestion and had sought advice from the experts, but she wasn't at all sure the words of wisdom had done her any good.

It was a long time before Nell was visited by sleep.

Chapter 6

Nell took a few sips of coffee before turning to the day's edition of the *Yorktide Daily Chronicle*. The big story that morning of December thirteenth was the grand re-opening of the dollar store in Wells. The event would feature the Silver Singers, a barbershop quartet whose members were all past seventy, and a professional balloon artist. Nell smiled—she hadn't been aware that one could be a professional balloon artist—and turned the page. The first thing that caught her eye was a large ad taken out by the Bookworm, Yorktide's independent bookshop.

> *We're thrilled to announce that* New York Times *best-selling novelist Eric Manville will be giving a reading at seven o'clock on the evening of December fifteenth. Doors open at six-fifteen. The first ten people through the door will receive a signed copy of Mr. Manville's latest novel,* The Land of Joy.

There was a picture, too, a professional photo of the famous and beloved author. There was the so familiar slightly crooked smile; there were the large, dark eyes, so soulful in expression; there was the unruly dark hair. "Eric," Nell whispered. She felt a strange tingling from head to toe. Only the day before she had twice thought with bittersweet nostalgia of Eric Manville. It seemed a very odd coincidence to find his name and picture in the morning paper. But of course it could be nothing other than coincidence.

Still, it struck Nell as odd that a *New York Times* best-selling author of popular novels, several of which had been made into successful movies starring big-name actors, would be doing an event in a virtually unknown little town in southern Maine in the middle of winter when there were no tourists to fill seats and stimulate sales. It couldn't be that . . . Nell felt her cheeks flush. Could Eric have learned that she lived in Yorktide? Could he be coming here to see her? The possibility was remote but not completely out of the question. Was it?

Nell frowned down at the page. No. She had broken Eric's heart when she abruptly ended their relationship in their senior year of college. There was no way he would want anything to do with her. Besides, Nell had read that he was married to a journalist who traveled the globe covering exciting stories in dangerous locations. Katrina Sinclair, whose picture was often to be found on the Internet as she was snapped accepting a prestigious award or interviewing harassed soldiers behind enemy lines, was tall and willowy with exotic dark eyes and a keen fashion sense. She was not the sort of woman from whom a man would easily stray, and Nell knew that Eric was not the sort of man even to contemplate a betrayal.

Even if Eric were single, Nell thought, what would a worldly, wealthy writer ever find attractive in Nell King at this point in time? She had done nothing particularly brilliant with her life. Correction. She had done nothing at *all* brilliant. Sure, since becoming office manager for Mutts and Meows she had upgraded the practice's website and overhauled the billing system, and back when she was married and in charge of the country club's annual charity ball she had routinely raised thousands of dollars over the club's stated goal, but none of that was worthy of a headline. Add to those mediocre accomplishments the fact that she hadn't aged particularly well and, Nell thought, you had a spectacularly average person on your hands. She had gained more weight than she felt comfortable carrying. She hadn't bothered to eliminate the gray hairs that were creeping into view or to address the issue of the deepening lines around her mouth. Not like the old days when she had spent endless amounts of time on her appearance in an effort to uphold her status as Joel King's perfect wife.

But long before *those* days, Nell thought, there had been Eric, a high-minded dreamer, aimless and happy-go-lucky. Intelligent, yes. A good student, no. Kind hearted. Generous. Gregarious, though someone who also appreciated the beauty and necessity of silence. It had taken about a moment for Nell and Eric to fall madly in love. It had taken about a month for them to decide they would marry after graduation.

All might have been well if it weren't for the fact that Nell's parents thought Eric unacceptable, and as soon as they realized their daughter's intention of marrying him, they mounted a campaign to undermine the relationship. "He's too bohemian for the likes of us," Jacqueline Emerson declared. "He has no firm plans for his future," Talbot Emerson added. "I want someone stable and ambitious for my daughter." And that someone was Joel King, son of Mr. Emerson's business partner.

In the end Nell simply hadn't been strong enough to

withstand her parents' formidable will; she never had been. She broke up with Eric. She started to date Joel. They married, and soon after the wedding Nell stopped writing poetry; soon after Molly's birth she stopped reading it, too. She had once known how to access the state of mind and heart that preceded both proper reading and writing, but those skills belonged to her old life. A life before marriage and motherhood.

Nell's memories were interrupted by the appearance of Molly in the doorway to the kitchen. Around her neck she wore a silver pendant that had been a gift from Mick on her sixteenth birthday. It seemed an odd choice given Molly's decision to end the relationship.

"I spoke to your father last night," Nell said, closing the newspaper. "I told him about your plans."

"Why did you do that?" Molly asked with a frown as she took a seat at the table and reached for the pitcher of grapefruit juice.

"Because I needed to."

"What did he say about my moving to Boston? Assuming he even cares."

"Of course he cares, and frankly, he's as puzzled as I am. Still, he offered to help fund you until you're settled and have a good job. And he said you could stay at his apartment."

Molly's expression grew hard. "I won't take his money or stay in his home."

Nell restrained a sigh. "You could at least admit it was good of him to offer to help you."

"Dad thinks all problems can be solved with money."

"That's unfair," Nell said sharply.

Molly reached for her mother's hand. "Look, Mom, there's a reason I haven't spoken to him since I turned eighteen. I don't like what he did to you. He treated you badly, and I'm not letting him off the hook so easily."

"I appreciate your loyalty, Molly, I really do, but it hurts me that you won't even listen to what he might have to say to you. I've forgiven him. Why can't you?"

Molly withdrew her hand. "I'm sorry, Mom. I don't want you to feel bad, but I just can't."

Nell decided to drop the subject of reconciliation. To the young, the world was black-and-white. The young were notoriously unsympathetic and couldn't be expected to be otherwise.

"You're still going ahead with your plans?" she said instead.

"Nothing has changed overnight, Mom."

"All right. But since you confided in me in the first place I'm asking you to hear me out."

Molly nodded. "I guess I can't stop you."

"No," Nell said. "You can't. Molly, there are a lot of good reasons to end a relationship, and a lot of bad ones, too. Be very certain breaking up is what you want to do. Some mistakes can't be corrected." *And I should know,* Nell added silently, glancing at the newspaper on the table. Eric Manville.

Molly sighed. "I know that, Mom. I do. It's just that I don't want to be someone who gives up her life just to be a wife and mother, and that's what will happen if I marry Mick. I'll be . . . I'll be *consumed* by Mick and his parents and the farm. I'll be Molly Williams of Williams Family Farm. I won't have any identity apart from them. I won't be *me*."

"You could look at the situation and see servitude rather than a partnership," Nell agreed. "But I think you're being unfair in assuming that Mick would be unwilling to respect your concerns. You block out all sort of possibilities when you assume someone is going to react a certain way."

"He won't understand my position," Molly replied flatly.

"He *loves* you," Nell insisted. "Even if he doesn't understand at first, he'll *try* to understand. I know he will."

"You can't know that."

Nell sighed. "Okay, maybe I can't. But sometimes it's wiser to cherish what you have instead of tossing it aside for some unknown, supposedly better thing. Sometimes what you really want is right in front of you. You just have to blink a few times to clear the smoke other people are blowing in your face."

"No one is blowing smoke in my face, and I'm not going to change my mind, Mom. There's nothing new for me with Mick. I know exactly what he's going to say and do next. He's so *predictable*. How can I spend the rest of my life with someone I know better than I know myself?"

"Just because you think you know someone doesn't mean he won't surprise you," Nell said carefully. "We all change over time. We surprise each other and ourselves over and over again."

"Did Dad surprise you when he said he was leaving you for his mistress?"

For a moment Nell wasn't quite sure how to answer honestly. "He did surprise me," she said finally. "But maybe I shouldn't have been surprised. Maybe I should have seen certain signs beforehand. But this conversation is not about your father and me. This is about you and Mick. What about the silver money clip you were planning on giving him for Christmas? You can't give it to him and then end the relationship."

"I'll return it. I'll get something less personal."

"You can't return it. It's monogrammed with both your initials."

"It's just a thing, Mom," Molly cried. "Why are you getting all worked up about a *thing*?"

"I'm not getting all worked up," Nell protested. And then she sighed. She suddenly felt exhausted. "How was dinner at the Williamses' last night?" she asked wearily.

Molly got up from the table. "Fine. I've got to go to class."

"You haven't eaten anything."

"I'm okay. I'll see you later."

And then she was gone. Nell sighed again. She doubted the evening had been "fine." Even if Mick and Gus hadn't picked up on anything amiss in Molly's mood, Mary Williams must have sensed that something was wrong. Women usually did, especially when it in some way involved their children.

So why didn't I sense that something was troubling Molly? Nell wondered guiltily. *Have I been so obsessed with the idea of my own impending loneliness that I've been ignoring signs of trouble brewing in the here and now?*

Nell opened the newspaper again. She stared at Eric Manville's image, and for a moment she had the distinct and disturbing feeling that he was looking back at her, about to speak to her, about to say . . . Nell abruptly closed the paper and shook her head. She had to keep her wits about her this Christmas if she was to provide her daughters with an experience they would never, ever forget.

Even when they were long gone from Yorktide.

Chapter 7

"Hey, did you see in the paper this morning that Eric Manville is doing a reading at the Bookworm?" Jill asked. "He's such a big name I can't understand why his publisher would waste their time sending him to Yorktide in the middle of winter."

Nell, who was stirring a bowl that contained large quantities of butter, sugar, and eggs, nodded. "I saw the announcement," she said. And without forethought she added, "I knew him once, you know."

"No," Jill said. "I didn't know. When?"

Nell stopped stirring the batter. She hadn't planned on sharing her secret, but the events of the last twenty-four hours had rattled her. *Why not,* she thought. *What does it matter now?* "I've never told this to anyone before," she said. "Eric and I met in college and fell in love. We were going to get married. I was going to be a poet. At the time, Eric had no idea what he wanted to do with his life other than to . . . Other than to be with me."

Jill sank into a seat at the table. "Wow," she said. "This is huge. What happened?"

Nell sighed. "I broke it off. I allowed my parents to talk

me out of the relationship. They had a different path in mind for me, one that didn't involve someone they saw as a dreamer with no real direction."

"A path that *did* involve Joel King?" Jill asked shrewdly.

"Yes. But to Joel's credit he wasn't complicit in my parents' campaign. All he knew was that I'd once had a friend named Eric Manville." Nell began to stir the batter again. "I'll never forget this," she went on. "Years later, after Eric had shot to fame, we were having dinner and one of the girls was gushing about the young actor in the movie version of one of his books. Joel turned to me and said something like, 'You knew that guy back in college, didn't you? I bet you wish you'd married him instead of me.' It was a joke, but it hit a sore spot."

"I'll say. So, *do* you regret not marrying Eric Manville?" Jill asked.

"Yes," Nell said. "I do regret not marrying Eric, but I don't regret marrying Joel. Without Joel I would never have had Molly and Felicity. And Joel was a good husband until he wasn't. He treated me well, though after the fact I realized he'd regarded me more as a junior partner than as an equal. But maybe I had something to do with establishing that dynamic."

Jill shook her head. "You're the most forgiving ex-wife I've ever known."

Nell thought about that observation for a moment. She had indeed long ago forgiven Joel for betraying their marriage vows. Not that his leaving had been anything like a relief; it had come as a total and horrifying shock. But it hadn't destroyed her, and it wasn't too long before she understood why. Joel wasn't Eric. He had never touched her in the way Eric Manville had. She had never fully given Joel her heart, so there had been no way for him to break it.

"I forgave him for the sake of my children," Nell said finally. It wasn't a lie, just not the entire truth.

"And you really never told anyone about this long-ago romance?" Jill asked.

"No," Nell admitted. "My parents, of course, never mentioned the name Eric Manville after I broke things off with him, especially not after he became famous. They had been entirely wrong about him, and no doubt it rankled."

"Good," Jill said firmly. "They should feel rotten for butting in. So, are you going to go to the reading at the Bookworm?"

"I want to," Nell said, "but I'm scared. I haven't seen Eric since just before we graduated, and it wasn't a happy scene. Just looking at his photo in the paper I felt kind of dizzy and disoriented."

"I could go with you for moral support," Jill suggested. "And you don't *have* to go up to him afterwards."

"I suppose."

"Still, if you do decide to go, you should ask yourself what you expect to get out of the encounter. I mean, it wouldn't be wise to harbor a fantasy of his taking you in his arms and declaring undying love."

Nell laughed. "Undying love! I have absolutely no hope or expectation of *that*."

"Okay. But a lot of memories might be stirred up. I think you should be prepared to feel sad. Just saying."

"And yet you think I should go to the reading?" Nell asked.

Jill shook her head. "I think it's your decision to make. And what was that about your being a poet? What happened there?"

"Nothing," Nell said firmly. "Nothing."

A clattering of heels racing down the stairs announced that Felicity was making her way to the kitchen.

"Don't say anything about what I just told you," Nell whispered. Jill nodded just as Felicity appeared in the doorway.

"I was just reading fondue recipes online," she announced. "The hotel we're staying at in Switzerland next Christmas serves traditional fondue made with Gruyère and Emmentaler and white wine and kirsch. Yum. I think I'll order that every night."

"You might get bored," Nell said lamely.

"Not to mention clog your arteries," Jill said with an arched eyebrow.

Felicity shrugged. "I'm young. My arteries don't matter yet. So, Mom, what are we having for dinner? That casserole you made last week really was awesome, the one with celeriac and parsnips and the breadcrumbs on top. Can we have that again soon?"

Nell smiled. "Sure. I'm glad you liked it."

"Well," Jill announced rising from the table. "I'm off. One of my former employees and I are going to see the new zombie film and then have dinner at the Chinese place on Route One."

Nell shuddered. "I don't know how you can watch that sort of thing. I caught *The Walking Dead* once for about a minute and had nightmares for weeks. But have fun."

Jill left with an assurance that she *would* have fun, and Nell began to form the dough she had been working on into one-inch balls.

"What's that for?" Felicity asked, pointing to a large folded piece of sky-blue felt that sat on the table next to a hot glue gun, a craft knife, a pair of super sharp scissors, and a stack of cardstock.

"I'm not quite sure," Nell admitted. "Either bookmarks in the shape of snowflakes or finger puppets in the shape of angels."

Felicity laughed. "Maybe you should quit your job at the vet's and become a kindergarten teacher! Well, I'm going to call Pam. I want to ask her about what sort of ski equipment I need to bring with me and what sort I can rent at the resort."

Felicity loped from the kitchen, leaving Nell alone with her baking. There was no sound but the low whirring of the oven and the distant ticking of the miniature grandfather clock in the living room. Nell glanced toward the stack of cookbooks lined on a shelf by the fridge. In her copy of Sarah Leah Chase's *Cold Weather Cooking* she had secreted the Bookworm's ad for Eric Manville's reading. Nell bit her lip. She wanted to drop what she was doing and stare hard at the image of her first and only love. But she resisted the urge. There was the baking to finish and dinner to prepare. Those were the more important things.

Chapter 8

"What are you baking today, Mom?" Felicity asked the next morning, taking a seat at the kitchen table with a bowl of cold cereal and a glass of juice.

Nell looked up from her breakfast. "How did you know I was planning to bake?" she asked.

"Because every single day this month you've baked cookies or tarts or bars."

"Don't forget pies and cakes and breads," Molly added.

"I haven't baked every single day," Nell protested.

"Yup," Felicity said. "Well, okay, there was that one day you had a migraine and didn't get out of bed, but other than that . . ."

"Don't you find coming home to the smell of gingerbread and cinnamon and chocolate comforting?"

Felicity shrugged. "Yeah, sure. I guess."

"Good. Today I thought I'd make Linzer sandwich cookies and pfeffernüse. But I have to pop out to the store first because I'm out of powdered sugar."

"I'm not surprised you're out of powdered sugar," Molly said, pouring more coffee into her cup. "The way you were mounding it on those butter cookies yesterday."

Felicity frowned. "Mom, how much money are you spending on all this stuff?"

"We're perfectly within budget," Nell said, a bit defensively.

Felicity got up from the table and went to the small pantry off the kitchen. A moment later she returned with a precariously balanced stack of cookie tins. "There's no way we can eat all of this! Let me bring a few of these tins to one of the local food banks."

"And I can make up a basket to take to school," Molly added. "The admin staff in the psych department will appreciate it."

Nell felt a little bit foolish. She also felt a little bit angry, a feeling she knew was not justified. "Sure," she said with feigned nonchalance. "Take what you want."

The doorbell sounded, and Nell got to her feet. "I'll get it," she said. A moment later she opened the front door to find Molly's boyfriend.

"Mick," she said with the automatic smile the sight of the young man always summoned. "Come in."

Mick followed Nell into the house. It was the first time Nell had seen him since Molly's announcement that she was ending the relationship, and now, after the first flush of pleasure at his presence, Nell felt almost as if she were the one betraying him.

"Morning Mrs. King," Mick said. "I'm sorry it's so early, but I've been up since four with one of the cows. We almost lost her back in the autumn to bloat, and ever since then I've been keeping a super close eye on her. My father thinks I'm being too cautious but, well, Mabel is one of my favorites."

"It's perfectly all right," Nell told him. "You're always welcome." And then she realized that before too much longer Mick would not indeed be welcome at the King home, and she felt even more duplicitous.

"I thought I heard your voice!" Felicity came dashing into the living room, followed more slowly by her sister, and threw herself into Mick's arms.

"Ooof!" Mick said with a laugh.

Mick Williams was a tall, broad-shouldered young man, powerfully built and the proverbial picture of health, from his ruddy cheeks to his thick, sandy hair. He was a person of common sense and practicality, yet not without a sensitive soul. Nell felt her heart break watching his face light up as he gave Molly a kiss.

"What's that?" Molly asked.

From the gift bag Mick held he extracted a scroll tied with a red ribbon. "This," he said, handing the scroll to Molly, "is an illustrated copy of the lyrics to 'The Twelve Days of Christmas.' On each of the twelve days between now and Christmas I'm going to bring you a present." Mick reached into the bag again and removed a wrapped package about four inches square. "Here's today's present," he said, "and on Christmas there's going to be a really big surprise."

"What's the surprise?" Felicity asked excitedly.

Mick laughed. "If I told you it wouldn't *be* a surprise!"

"I promise I won't tell Molly. Just whisper it to me."

Molly scowled at her sister. "Fliss, stop it."

"It's all right," Mick said good-naturedly. Then he kissed Molly on the cheek. "I've got to run," he said. " 'Bye, Mrs. King, bye, Felicity."

"Goodbye, Mick," Nell said. She closed the door behind him and turned to her daughters.

"You know, the twelve days of Christmas are the ones *after* the twenty-fifth," Felicity pointed out. "Still, what Mick's doing is sweet. Don't you think it's sweet, Molly?"

Molly nodded. Her expression had become alarmingly blank.

"So, what's in the package?" Nell asked.

Molly looked down at the package in her hand as if she wasn't sure how it had gotten there. Slowly she unwrapped it. "It's a pack of *Partridge Family* collectible cards," she said. "For a partridge in a pear tree, I guess."

"Cool," Felicity said. "They might be valuable if they're originals from the seventies. Mick's awesome. Well, I'll be late for school if I don't get out of here now. Bye!"

Felicity grabbed her coat and bag from where they were flung over the back of an easy chair and hurried from the house. Nell waited for her older daughter to speak.

"I can't believe he's doing this," Molly said finally.

"What?" Nell asked. "Treating you well? You've got to talk to him, Molly. It would be cruel to let him carry on with some grand romantic scheme when you're planning to break up with him."

Molly didn't reply. She put the stack of collectible cards on an end table.

Nell sighed. "Have you thought about how breaking up with Mick will affect your relationship with Gus and Mary?"

"What do you mean?" Molly asked.

"Well, if you're going to end things with Mick you'll be ending your relationship with his parents, too. Maybe years down the line relations could be amicable, but you certainly won't be having dinner with them once a week like you've been doing for the past six years."

Molly laughed grimly. "Are you saying I should stay with Mick so that I don't upset his parents?"

"Of course not, Molly," Nell replied. "But no relationship exists in isolation, especially not in a small community like ours. I just want you to be aware of how lots of things will change if you and Mick part ways. Your mutual friends might take sides as the easiest way to handle the new situation. You'll have to accept that and not be angry with them."

"You could still be friends with Mr. and Mrs. Williams," Molly argued.

"Molly. It's not that simple." Nell resisted the impulse to rub her temples. It was difficult to believe her daughter could be so naïve or so willfully ignorant of the effects of what she was so poorly planning to do. Hadn't those psychology courses she had been taking for the past four years taught her anything?

"I don't want to talk about it anymore, Mom," Molly said suddenly. "I've got to go. Call me later if you need me to get anything from the store on my way home from school."

When Molly had gone, Nell picked up the scroll that had somehow found its way to the couch, removed the ribbon, and unrolled the song sheet. Just as Mick had told them, its borders were decorated with colorful images from lords a-leaping to maids a-milking. Nell shook her head. It must have cost Mick a pretty penny, money he could have spent more wisely if only he had known that the recipient of his thoughtfulness would be unappreciative.

Nell returned the scroll to the couch, and with a troubled sigh she prepared to leave for a half day at Mutts and Meows.

Chapter 9

Later that afternoon Jill stopped by to return a book she had borrowed. She had been in the house only a moment before Nell told her about Mick's "Twelve Days of Christmas" scheme, to which Jill replied: "Ouch. This could very well be a train wreck."

"Felicity thinks it's sweet, and of course so would I in other circumstances. I don't know what to do," Nell admitted. "My heart broke watching Mick all excited and Molly standing there like a statue."

"There's nothing you can do," Jill pointed out. "This is Molly's potential train wreck, not yours."

"Yes, but you know how it is when your child is making a mess of things. The urge to step in and fix everything is so strong."

"I certainly do know," Jill said shortly. "That's a new apron, isn't it?"

"I couldn't resist. It was only three dollars, so I got matching ones for Molly and Felicity." Nell lifted the bottom of the apron and looked at the upside down images of chubby bunnies and pert-faced foxes wearing winter garb. "Kind of silly, I guess."

Jill shrugged. "Whatever makes you happy."

Nell looked closely at her friend. "Something's bothering you, isn't it?" she asked.

"Yeah," Jill said with a sigh. "I've been thinking about Brian all morning. I've been remembering the way he'd rattle the ice in his drink and the way his knee bounced when he was forced to sit for too long. Both habits used to drive me crazy, but I'd do anything to have Brian back, making my nerves stand on end."

"I'm sorry, Jill," Nell said with genuine sympathy.

"I suppose I should be thankful the end came so soon. Brian would have hated a long, drawn-out illness. Still, it seems so unbelievably unfair . . . But why should death be fair? Life isn't. Anyway, this is the first Christmas in seventeen years I'll be without him. I'd be lying if I said it's going to be easy. I'll miss the old routine of Brian going to see Charlie in Augusta, my going to see Stuart in Connecticut, and our reuniting the day after Christmas to celebrate, just the two of us."

"At least you'll be spending time with Stuart." Nell grimaced. "Sorry. One person doesn't replace another. I don't know why I said that."

"It's okay. Anyway, Charlie sent me a lovely Christmas card with a heartfelt message thanking me for being so good to his father through the years we were together. It made me cry, and I don't cry easily." Jill nodded toward the counter. "On another note, what's that you're hiding?"

Nell lifted the large dishtowel that was covering a baking pan. "I made gingerbread people."

Jill peered down at the pan. "This one looks suspiciously like me."

"It's meant to. See the yellow dots around her neck? That's the strand of citrine beads you bought in Portland last month."

Jill put a hand to the silver-and-lapis necklace she was wearing that afternoon. "I didn't know my jewelry had become a hallmark."

"Your jewelry is one of your signatures. And this one is Molly and this one is Fliss."

"Obvious from the glasses and the ponytail respectively. So, where's the cookie that's meant to be you?"

Nell laughed awkwardly. "It never occurred to me make one in my own likeness," she said. And she wondered why. Was it a mother's ingrained habit of self-effacement? Or was it something else, a long-standing inability to accord herself the respect and recognition she was due as a unique individual, not just someone's daughter, wife, or mother? *What are my signatures?* she wondered. *What do people see when they look at me? What do they remember when I'm gone?*

"Nice work with the icing, by the way," Jill said, interrupting Nell's unsettling musings.

"I made it from scratch and used food coloring to get exactly the shades I wanted."

Jill laughed. "Better woman than I am. Are we actually supposed to eat these cookies? I'm not sure how I feel about biting off my own head, or Molly's or Felicity's for that matter."

"I hadn't really thought about anyone eating them. You could take an anonymous gingerbread person instead," Nell suggested.

"I think I'll pass on devouring anyone, thanks. I've been eating enough sugar these days. Those butter cookie sandwiches with chestnut cream almost did me in."

"They were pretty decadent, weren't they? But they weren't a big hit with the girls."

"Maybe they're sated, too."

Nell looked down at the baking pan of gingerbread figures. *Sated* might be another way of saying the girls were
fed up. Bored. Ready to move on.

"Don't you think you're overcompensating just a wee
bit this holiday season?" Jill asked quietly.

"Overcompensating for what?" Nell asked, looking
back to her friend, aware of her defensive tone.

"Let me rephrase the question. Don't you think you
might be trying a bit too hard to prove to the girls that
Christmas here at home with you is better than Christmas
in the Swiss Alps or in Boston or indeed anywhere else
they might choose to wander?"

For a moment Nell didn't reply. There had been mention of overcompensating behaviors on a few of those
websites dedicated to dealing with empty nest syndrome.
There had been mention of a tendency in the mother an-
ticipating a child's departure to ignore her own needs and
desires more so than she ever had before. *No Christmas
decorations in my room,* Nell thought. *No cookie in my
image. No . . .*

"Maybe I *am* overcompensating a little," Nell said finally, "but what's wrong with trying to make this Christmas truly memorable?"

Jill shook her head. "Sorry. There's nothing wrong with
it, and I have no right to judge when my one concession to
holiday decorations has always only been a single white
candle in every window. So, are you still on for the reading
tomorrow night? I'll drive."

"Sure," Nell said with more confidence than she felt.
And she was grateful that Jill had offered to drive. She
wasn't at all sure what kind of state she would be in after
the reading, a weeping, nostalgic mess, devoid of any feeling at all, overcome by regret. Whatever state she was in, it

probably would not be conducive to getting them home safely.

"Maybe I'll take the gingerbread me after all," Jill said suddenly. "I'll bite off my own head so no one else has to."

Nell managed a smile. "Thanks, Jill," she said.

"For what?" Jill asked.

"For keeping me honest."

Chapter 10

"**D**o you like the chicken?" Nell asked that evening as she and her daughters were at the table. "It's one of Julia Child's recipes."

Felicity, whose mouth was full, nevertheless managed to mumble something that sounded like, "'Sgood." Molly nodded.

"Pam said the photo shoot for the watch company went really well," Felicity announced suddenly. "The stylist works with some of the cast of that new science fiction show on HBO, and she once dressed an A-lister for the Oscars. Can you believe it? Pam said she couldn't tell me the name of the A-lister for some reason, but anyway, she's sending me her old Rolex by FedEx."

"Why do you need a Rolex?" Molly asked with a frown. "Do you know how much it costs to maintain those things? Basically she's sending you a bill."

Felicity sighed. "Can't you ever admit that Pam is a decent person? You always find something negative to say about her. You always suspect her motives."

Molly made no reply.

"Be sure to send Pam a thank you note," Nell advised, "and not just an email or a text."

"Okay. Hey, I wonder what Mick will bring by tomorrow. I mean how is he going to handle turtledoves? I don't even know what they are really, besides some sort of bird."

Molly shrugged.

"Aren't you curious?" Felicity asked her sister.

"Not really," Molly said. "I mean, I'll find out in the morning."

"I'm *dying* to know. The whole thing is so romantic."

Romantic, Nell thought. Like the things Eric Manville used to do for her. She remembered how he would slip humorous messages of encouragement into the notebook she used for a course she found particularly difficult. She remembered how he would drive to a bakery three towns away to get her the cinnamon donuts she loved. She remembered—

"Mom?"

Nell startled. Felicity was looking at her curiously. "What?"

"I just said that those gingerbread cookies you made look amazing. But where's the one that's supposed to be you?"

"I didn't make one," she said with forced nonchalance.

"Why not?" Molly asked.

Nell shrugged, and then some small perverse impulse made her ask: "If you were going to make a cookie that people would recognize as me at first glance, what would it look like?"

"I don't know," Felicity admitted after a moment. "You're just you. You know, you're just Mom."

Nell managed a small smile. "Molly?" she asked.

"You know I'm not creative," Molly said. "Besides, Fliss is right. You're just Mom."

Nell took a bite of chicken, but it tasted like ashes in her mouth. When had she become so much a part of the woodwork, so taken for granted that she was now in effect invisible? *But isn't that what I've always wanted,* Nell wondered as she chewed, *to be so integral a part of my children they hardly know that I'm there?* But at that moment, being indistinguishable didn't feel like such a good thing after all.

Chapter 11

"Would you grab the paper?" Nell asked her older daughter the next morning when they had finished breakfast and were gathered in the living room. "It wasn't there earlier. Our paperboy must be running late."

Molly went to the door and a moment later returned with the *Yorktide Daily Chronicle* under her left arm and a square box wrapped in bright green paper in her right hand.

"From Mick?" Nell asked unnecessarily.

Molly nodded.

"I wonder why he didn't ring the bell," Felicity said. "He was probably in a hurry. Well, aren't you going to open it?"

Molly dropped the newspaper onto an end table and slowly removed the green wrapping paper. In the box and carefully nestled in tissue paper was a Wedgwood blue Jasperware disk ornament depicting the image of a turtle-dove. Threaded through the top of the ornament was a white silk string with a tassel.

"It's lovely," Nell said.

"It is," Felicity agreed. "You know, I bet you're going to

miss Mick when you're having a wild and crazy time in Boston."

"I didn't say it's going to be wild and crazy," Molly said testily.

"No," Felicity agreed. "You're not the nightclub type. In fact, I think you're going to miss Mick *so* much you'll decide to come home after a few weeks. Why don't you just move to Portland instead of Boston? Portland's only like forty minutes away, and it's a lot less expensive than Boston. It would be way less of a hassle to move there and back."

Nell restrained a sigh. Now she felt as if she were betraying her younger daughter by allowing her to go on blithely as she was, assuming that nothing in her sister's life had changed while the reality was something quite different.

Molly closed the lid of the box and put it on the end table next to the newspaper. "Don't mention my going to Boston when you see Mick, okay?" she said, ignoring her sister's suggestion.

"Why?" Felicity asked. "Is he upset that you're going?"

"Let's just respect Molly's wishes," Nell said quickly.

Felicity shrugged. "Sure."

"So," Nell went on, "haven't either of you noticed the crèche I set up last night?" She gestured toward a small end table on which sat a three-sided wooden barnlike structure with a thatched roof. At the apex of the roof, which stood about nine inches from the base of the structure, Nell had attached the figure of an angel holding aloft an undulating banner proclaiming "Peace on Earth."

"I bought it the last time I was in Portland," she said. "The Nativity is such a sweet scenario. What's lovelier than a newborn baby and his mother?"

Felicity went over to the scene and picked up the figure

of an older man carrying a staff. "Don't forget Joseph," she said, moving the figure closer to the baby in his cradle of hay. "The father is a big part of the story, even though he's not technically the father."

"Yes," Nell said, with a twinge of guilt. Had she been aware of excluding the father from the heart of the scene? "The father, too. I know we've never had a crèche before, but I thought it would be a nice addition to our home."

Molly shrugged. "Whatever. It's your house, Mom, you can do what you want."

Nell felt stricken. "No," she said. "It's *our* house. It's *our* home."

"You know what I mean," Molly said. "Fliss and I won't be living here forever. I'd better get going." Molly reached for her backpack and coat, both flung across a chair.

"Aren't you going to put Mick's gift somewhere safe?" Nell asked.

Molly, at the front door, looked briefly over her shoulder. "It's fine where it is," she said. In a moment she was gone.

"What's up with her these days?" Felicity asked. "She's never been moody and short-tempered, except for the time she had that really bad flu that took forever to go away."

Nell picked up the box with its green wrapping paper still partly attached. "She's under a lot of strain with school," she said evasively. "I'll put this under the tree."

"Well, whatever's bothering her, I hope she gets over it before Christmas. Oh, I almost forgot," Felicity cried. "I know I said I'd go to the Christmas fair at Saint Pat's with you later, but I can't."

"Why not?" Nell asked. "We go every year."

"The thing is I'm going to the fair with a bunch of girls from school instead. Don't be mad, okay? It's just that after the fair we're going down to the outlets in Kittery."

Nell didn't see what one thing had to do with the other, but she didn't argue. "Sure," she said, managing a smile.

Felicity grinned. "Thanks, Mom. Bye."

And then Felicity was gone as well, the front door slamming behind her.

Alone, Nell suddenly had the strange feeling that the grinning faces of the cherub figurines that sat on either end of the mantel were mocking her. She wanted so badly to make this Christmas perfect but try as she might, her efforts didn't seem to be garnering the results she had hoped for. *And what results are those?* Nell asked herself. *My daughters declaring they'll never grow up and leave me?* With a shake of her head, Nell strode from the living room.

Chapter 12

When the girls had gone off after dinner Nell snuck a look at the newspaper ad she had stashed in her copy of *Cold Weather Cooking*. She no longer had the impression that Eric Manville was trying to say something to her or that he was actually seeing her, and she was glad about that. It had been a silly notion, most likely brought on by the shock of learning that he would be in town in a matter of days.

She had returned the ad to its hiding place and gone to her room to change. She took special care in dressing, though she remembered that Eric had never bothered about clothes and other outward trappings. But that was a long time ago. Fame might have changed him in so many ways. For all she knew he might look at her and see not only a stranger but a poorly dressed one at that, one to whom time had been cruel.

Would he be angry she had shown up at the reading? Or would he be unaffected by her presence? Nell's stomach was in knots thinking about these questions. If she hadn't told Jill about her past with Eric, she would back out of the plan to attend the reading. If she cancelled now Jill would call her on her cowardice, and Nell didn't have the energy for an argument.

At precisely six-thirty Jill pulled up to the house. "You look very spiffy," she said as Nell slid into the passenger seat of her black Volvo.

"I'm not trying to impress anyone if that's what you're implying."

Jill raised an eyebrow. "I wasn't implying anything. I was sharing my opinion of your spiffiness."

"Sorry," Nell said. "Guess I'm a little nervous. In fact I did take care getting dressed tonight."

"Did the girls notice?"

"Molly is babysitting and Felicity was in her room doing homework when I left. I told them I was going out with you, but neither asked where."

"Sometimes the self-centeredness of the young can be a blessing," Jill noted.

A blessing or a curse, Nell thought, remembering that at dinner Felicity hadn't bothered to ask if her mother had gone to the Christmas fair at St. Pat's on her own. In fact, Nell had not.

Ten minutes later Jill pulled into the last space available in the lot belonging to the Bookworm. "Looks like a full house tonight," she commented.

"Here goes nothing," Nell said under her breath, but not quietly enough to escape Jill's notice.

"Ditch the negative attitude, Nell," she advised. "It doesn't go with your outfit."

The moment Jill opened the door to the shop they were greeted with the loud and happy noise of a crowd that had come together for a common purpose. There was laughter and excited chatter as people greeted one another and vied for the few remaining seats. "Over here," Jill shouted, and Nell followed her to the last two empty chairs. Nell realized gratefully that they would be partly hidden from the vantage point of the old wooden podium the Bookworm's owner, Bruce Lewis, had purchased from the local library when it was being refurbished a few years back.

Jill turned to answer a question posed by the woman seated on her other side, and it was then that Nell saw Eric. He was talking to Bruce Lewis, his hands shoved into the front pockets of his dark jeans. An unbidden smile came to Nell's lips, and she felt tenderness flood her heart. She remembered that habit. She tried to look at Eric objectively but knew that wasn't possible. He was just five feet eight inches tall, still as slim and wiry as he had been in college. His cheekbones were sharp; his lips delicately curved; his eyes large and brown. His hair was still wild and loosely curly. Nell had always found his appearance to be highly Romantic. She had always thought that if he were an actor he would be perfect in the role of Percy Bysshe Shelley. Over his dark sweater Eric was wearing a well-worn leather jacket. A long scarf was looped twice around his neck. Eric had always been cold, Nell remembered. Even in the summer he had often worn a sweater, usually a ratty old thing.

Bruce Lewis stepped up to the podium now, and the crowd quieted. He announced Eric with little fanfare, and Eric took his place at the podium. He smiled at the crowd gathered to hear him read, and Nell found that her hands were clasped so tightly together that they hurt.

"You okay?" Jill whispered.

Nell nodded. In fact she was not okay. The moment Eric began to read from his latest novel, Nell found herself transported to her past. Instead of seeing Eric at the wooden podium she saw him on the campus quad, tossing a Frisbee with his friends. She felt his lips meeting hers fiercely, tenderly. She heard his easy and frequent laughter as they strolled around the campus arm in arm, talking about everything and nothing. She watched as her hand caressed his cheek. She—

A sudden burst of applause brought Nell abruptly out of the sort of memory trance into which she had fallen when Eric had begun to read. She realized that she had hardly heard a word, only the sound of his voice, so familiar and yet so sadly alien, as the backdrop of her memories.

"That was wonderful," Jill said. "Wasn't it?"

Again, Nell nodded but she felt emotionally drained, utterly depleted, and terribly, terribly sad. *I can't face him,* she thought. *I just can't.* "Come on," she whispered to Jill as she rose from her seat. Jill rose, too, and they made their way to the central aisle.

"Nell!"

Nell froze for a second and then slowly turned, realizing that Jill was no longer by her side. She stood absolutely still as Eric approached through the throng. He stopped a few feet from her and smiled. "Imagine my surprise when I saw you in the audience," he said.

Nell laughed nervously. It was better than bursting into tears. "Imagine my surprise when I saw you'd be here in Yorktide."

"Mr. Manville!" A man came up to Eric and took his arm. "Could I ask you a question about your first book?"

Eric promised he would answer his question in a moment, and the man released him. He turned again to Nell. "Look," he said, lowering his voice, "could we meet somewhere privately tomorrow for lunch? I'm staying at the Starfish in Ogunquit."

"Of course," Nell said, surprised by his suggestion and amazed at her ability to answer coherently. "The Golden Apple is nice. I'm sure the staff at the Starfish can give you directions. One o'clock?"

Eric smiled and reached into his pocket. "Great. Here's my card with my contact information. Call me if something comes up and you have to reschedule." He turned back to the group that had been gathering behind him, and immediately several people began to voice questions and comments.

Carefully Nell put Eric's card in a small pocket inside her bag for safekeeping and scanned the shop for Jill. She spotted her by the entrance and made her way over.

"You okay?" Jill asked, looking searchingly at Nell.

"I think so."

Jill smiled. "Well, he certainly didn't forget you."

"No," Nell said. "He didn't forget."

"He's awfully attractive. There's something magnetic about him."

"Yes," Nell said. "Look, I'm ready to go if you are."

Jill nodded, and the two women went out into the frosty December night. "He wants to see me tomorrow," Nell blurted. "What do you think that means?"

Jill put her arm through Nell's. "I think," she said, "that it could mean anything. Come on. Let's go home."

Chapter 13

The sky was overcast, and for someone in Nell's state of mind this lent the night a feeling of romantic moodiness. Nell stood at her bedroom window, her robe pulled tightly around her. She had been home for more than two hours and yet still felt wrapped in the state of stunned and pleased surprise that had come over her on the drive back.

"I love him," she whispered to the winter night. It was true. What she felt was more than just the bittersweet pull of nostalgia. What she felt was *love*. It seemed impossible, even outrageous, but Nell knew what love felt like. She recognized it, even after all these years of it having lain dormant. No, her love for Eric hadn't died. It had just gone into hiding.

Nell turned from the window. She so hoped that her feelings hadn't shown on her face. The man was *married*, and Nell had always held the state of marriage in the highest regard. Besides, the last thing she wanted was to make a fool of herself in front of someone for whom she had always had the greatest respect. Maybe, she thought with a bit of a sinking feeling, it wasn't a good idea to meet him the next day. She might not be able to hide her emotions, and that would only result in an awkward disaster.

Nell sat on the edge of her bed. She would cancel their lunch date; she would tell Eric something urgent had come up. But . . . but this might very well be the last time she would have the opportunity to see Eric face-to-face. The only man she had ever truly loved. Nell sighed. The need to speak with him one more time before she got on with her soon to be post-parental life was too great to ignore. For better or worse she would meet him the following day, and she would school her emotions into obedience.

They would have lunch. They would trade basic information and trivialities, nothing more. And then Eric would go back to his wife and to their life together in New York City and she would continue doing . . . whatever it was she did. It would be enough to be in Eric's presence for an hour, to memorize his face at this moment in time, to commit to heart once again the sound of his voice and the shape of his hands and the color of his eyes, and then to say goodbye.

It would have to be enough.

Chapter 14

The moment Nell had taken a seat at her desk that morning Dr. Levy had stopped by to say that she had been at the reading the night before and had seen Nell in the audience. "It was wonderful, wasn't it?" Dr. Levy said. "He reads so well."

Nell agreed that Eric did indeed read well. Dr. Levy had then moved on to the lab; she had not said she had seen Nell speaking with Eric, and indeed, even if she had witnessed their brief conversation, she might well have assumed they had been discussing Eric's work, not arranging a private assignation.

Nell found herself blushing. Assignation? Really? No sooner had Dr. Levy gone than the senior vet technician, a gifted young woman named Heather, stopped at Nell's desk to deliver a file. "You're looking happy today, Nell," she said. "Getting into the holiday spirit?"

"I guess I am looking forward to Christmas," Nell admitted.

"It's always been my favorite time of the year," Heather said, "even if it has been overly commercialized. By the way, I saw Mick Williams on my way to work this morning. What a nice young man. You must be so pleased your daughter found such a gem."

Nell smiled, though she was pretty sure the smile didn't reach her eyes. "Yes," she said. "Mick is wonderful."

He had come by the house that morning with his third gift, a heavy linen dishcloth printed with the image of a sprightly hen. Molly had barely glanced at the cloth before stuffing it back into its wrapping and giving Mick a quick and very sisterly peck on the cheek. Luckily, Felicity hadn't been around to notice and comment on her sister's less than enthusiastic response. She had gone off early to deliver a tin of her mother's cookies to Yorktide's firehouse.

"Has Molly set a date for the wedding?" Heather asked. "I know they're not officially engaged yet, but I can't tell you how many people are looking forward to seeing those two get married."

"Not yet," Nell said, her smile faltering.

"Well—"

Just then the front door of the clinic opened and in rushed a man and woman, carrying between them a large dog wrapped in a blanket. "He was hit by a car!" the man cried, tears streaming down his face. Within seconds, Nell and Heather were helping the couple and their dog into one of the examination rooms. Dr. Levy and another technician came running from the lab, and all thoughts of anything but helping in what ways she could vanished from Nell's mind.

Nell sat behind the wheel of her car outside the tiny café on a rarely traveled road just beyond the large property owned by the Gascoyne family. She didn't know what sort of vehicle Eric might be driving; one of the two cars parked alongside her own might belong to him. Or he might not yet have arrived. Or he might not be coming at all. And if that proved to be the case, then only Jill would know her shame. Nell had told no one else about her lunch date.

Gathering her courage, Nell got out of the car and made her way into the Golden Apple. A quick glimpse told her that Eric was not there. It was five minutes past one. Nell was shown to a table for two. She sat and glanced again at her watch.

A few minutes later the door to the café opened with a rush of cold air. Nell looked up eagerly, but the man who had entered was not Eric. Another few minutes later and Nell was beginning to feel a bit pathetic. Just when self-pity was morphing into downright social embarrassment, the door opened again, and this time Eric Manville was indeed the person scanning the café. When he saw her he smiled and came hurrying over.

"I'm sorry I'm late," he said. "I got a bit lost. Reception gave me directions, but they went in one ear and out the other, and my GPS thing doesn't seem to be working. After going in circles for a while I finally stopped at a little grocery store and asked for directions. Turns out I was just down the road."

So much for the cliché of men never stopping to ask for directions, Nell thought. Then again, Eric always had been out of the ordinary. "It's all right," she said. "Finding your way around this part of the world takes some getting used to."

When Eric took off his coat, a bulky puffer that made him look like the Michelin man, Nell saw that he was wearing the same clothes he had worn the night before. She was not surprised that fame and money hadn't made him a diva.

"I'm starved," Eric announced. "What's good here?"

"Everything," Nell told him. "It's a family-run business so there's great quality control. Mom handles the financial end of things, Dad rules the kitchen, and the kids do the rest. That said, the fish chowder here is amazing."

The waitress, the daughter of the owner as Nell had mentioned, took their order—two bowls of fish chowder—and went off to the kitchen.

"Thanks for meeting me today," Eric said. He leaned forward and folded his hands on the table.

Nell nodded. She felt a bit disconcerted under his direct and penetrating gaze. "Sure," she said. "I mean it's my pleasure. It's good to see you. I thought . . ." Nell laughed nervously. "I suppose I thought I'd never see you again."

"Life is full of surprises." Eric smiled. "I won't say you haven't changed in twenty years because you have. You're lovelier than ever."

Nell shook her head. "Eric, please. I'm . . . I'm not."

"No, I mean it." His tone was earnest. "Experience has given you a certain patina. It's like you buy a shiny gold ring and it's lovely and you wear it through thick and thin, through good times and bad, and then you realize that now the ring glows in a softer, richer, deeper way."

Before Nell could frame a response to that observation—if there was a response to be found—the waitress brought their chowder.

"Are you still married?" Eric asked the moment she had gone off. "I heard about your marriage, of course. And yes, I know. I'm as blunt as I used to be back in college."

Blunt, Nell thought, *and entirely without pretense.* "No," she told him. "Joel and I have been divorced for some time. Our daughters live with me. Molly is a senior in college and Felicity is a senior in high school."

"I'm sorry about the divorce," Eric said feelingly. "So, why aren't you showing me pictures of your girls?"

Nell smiled and pulled her cell phone from her bag. "Molly is on the left," she said, handing the phone to Eric. "This was taken at Thanksgiving."

"I can see you in both of them," Eric noted. "In Molly the similarity is mostly around the eyes. In Felicity, there's something about her posture."

"You always were a keen observer of people," Nell noted as Eric returned the phone. "It must help with your writing."

"It does. What work do you do, Nell?"

Nell hesitated. She was proud of her job, but it wasn't what she had once dreamed of doing, and she worried that Eric might be disappointed in her. Then again, why would he care enough to feel anything other than polite interest in what she had become? "I'm the office manager at a veterinary clinic called Mutts and Meows," she said. "The team does amazing work. Just this morning Doctor Levy performed an emergency surgery that saved a dog's life. And we also help place animals in forever homes."

"And how do you fit into the team as office manager?" Eric asked.

"Well, I design and manage the website. I handle billing and help with staffing matters and keep track of office and medical supplies." Nell shrugged. "I'm just generally *there*. When that poor dog came in this morning Doctor Levy asked me to stay with his owners while he was in surgery and offer what comfort I could. That's the best part of the job by far, though it's definitely the most difficult."

"I'm impressed," Eric said. "Not only by the care-giving component of your work but by the business stuff as well. Technology and I aren't friends, and organization has never been a strong point." Eric grinned. "You probably know that."

Nell couldn't help but laugh. "I remember the time you lost ten pages of a twenty-page paper between one corner and the next. We searched every inch of that street for those missing pages, only to realize that somehow they had migrated from your hand to your backpack."

"Yeah, well, an irresponsible college kid is amusing but an irresponsible adult, not so much. I worked on getting my act together. I'm not entirely changed, but then I wouldn't want to be."

"I wonder if anyone can entirely change," Nell mused, "should he or she want to."

Eric shrugged. "Doubtful, but I'll leave that question to philosophers, theologians, and psychiatrists."

"Excuse me. Eric Manville?"

A nicely dressed middle-aged woman was standing by their table, her hands clasped in front of her in a gesture of supplication.

"Yes," Eric said with a smile. "That's me."

The woman leaned forward, and when she spoke her voice was almost a whisper. "I'm so sorry to bother you," she said. "But I wonder if I might have an autograph. I just love your books."

"Sure," Eric said, patting his pockets. "I'd be delighted. If I can find a pen . . ."

Nell held out the pen she always kept in her bag, and Eric reached for a napkin. "What's your name?" he asked the woman. "And will this napkin do?"

"Carol," she said. "Thank you so very much, anything will be fine."

Nell watched as Eric penned a note and signed his name. Then he handed the napkin to the woman, who thanked him again, practically curtsying in her gratitude.

"I'm sorry," Nell said when the woman had gone off. "I

thought this place would be out of the way enough so you wouldn't be bothered."

"I don't mind," Eric assured her. "Meeting a reader makes my day."

"Just part of the glamorous life of a famous novelist?"

Eric laughed. "There's nothing glamorous about living under a microscope. One time I was buying toilet paper in the local bodega and this man took a picture of me on his cell phone. I mean, who could possibly be interested in what brand of toilet paper I buy?"

"Did you say anything to him?" Nell asked.

"What could I say? I just paid for the toilet paper and left. I did look over my shoulder once or twice on the way back to my loft to see if he was following me, but he wasn't."

"Have you ever been really frightened by a fan?" Nell asked.

"Not at all," Eric said. "What scares me is failing to live up to the standards to which my readership holds me. People see my name on the cover of a book and they expect a certain level of quality. It's hard always trying to improve on what you've already accomplished. But at the same time it's a challenge, and without a challenge to keep you moving forward, well, where would you be?"

"Standing still." *Which is something I know an awful lot about,* Nell thought. "I've read a few of your wife's articles," she said. "I found them very perceptive and well written."

Eric nodded. "Katrina is an excellent investigative journalist, but she's no longer my wife. We've been divorced for two years. Katrina's contacts helped us keep the news out of the press."

"Oh," Nell said. After a moment she added: "I'm sorry." And she genuinely was sorry. But she was also not *that* sorry. She bent her head and took a spoonful of chowder, hoping very much that Eric, the observant writer, wouldn't be able to read the mixed emotions on her face.

"Thanks," he said evenly. "It was probably as amicable as a divorce can be. When you routinely don't see your spouse for months on end, well, not many relationships can survive that. Ours couldn't, though we stuck it out for ten years. That's a terrible thing to say, isn't it? You shouldn't be sticking out a marriage. You should be thriving in it. And before you ask, no, we had no children. I would have liked a family, but I knew from the start that Katrina wasn't interested. Who knows, maybe I just didn't want kids badly enough. If I had, maybe I would have made different choices. But that's all hindsight."

Hindsight. Different choices. You should be thriving in a marriage. Suddenly Nell felt desperately sad, much as she had the night before at the Bookworm when the reading had come to an end and she had come to her senses.

"I should get back to the office," she said abruptly, before the tears could begin to flow.

"Of course. And I should get back to my computer."

Eric paid their check and they went out to the cold and bright December day. Eric pointed at a vehicle that might charitably be called a beater. "I call her Mustang Sally," he said, "though she's about as far from a Mustang as she can get. I've never been into fancy cars. As long as it gets me where I'm going, it's fine by me."

"I remember that old VW bus you had in college," Nell told him. "One of the doors was held on by wire and a broken window was covered with duct tape."

"Yeah, it probably shouldn't have been on the road. When I tried to sell it for parts the mechanic just laughed at me. At least Sally's passed inspection."

Nell managed a smile. "It was good to see you again, Eric," she said. "Goodbye."

Eric frowned. "Didn't I mention that I'm staying on for a few weeks?"

"No," Nell said. Surprise made her almost shout the word. "You didn't."

"Really? I could have sworn I had. The thing is, I don't really have any reason to go home at the moment. Wait, that sounds pathetic. It's just that I've gotten out of the habit of celebrating holidays with anything other than take-out Chinese. With Katrina traveling so often Christmas sort of fell by the wayside, and with my own crazy schedule even my family doesn't expect me to show up until a week or two after the fact." Eric smiled. "So, I know you're busy, but maybe you could show me the sights?"

"You might be bored," Nell warned. "Yorktide is pretty quiet at all times, and even Ogunquit is a bit of a ghost town in winter."

"I won't be bored," Eric stated, pulling his cell phone from his pocket. "May I have your phone number?"

"Of course." Nell gave it to him and then put out her hand. "Well, goodbye for now."

"I think we're beyond handshakes," Eric said, and before Nell knew what was happening she was engulfed in his arms. Tears pricked at her eyes as she eased her arms around him.

When he released her he was smiling and Nell, blinking back a few tears, responded in kind. "Thanks," she said.

"Hope I didn't squish you with the coat. I found it in a thrift shop for thirty dollars, and it's the warmest thing I own. I figured it was the right thing to bring to Maine."

Nell laughed. "It is pretty . . . large."

"That it is. I'll call you, Nell. Goodbye."

Eric got in his car, pulled out of the lot, and turned in

the direction of Ogunquit. Nell got in her own car and headed toward Yorktide. Only when she had reached the clinic did the full reality of what had just transpired hit her. Eric was divorced. He was staying on. He wanted to see her again. Nell felt exhilarated. She felt terrified. She felt confused. But she no longer felt sad.

Chapter 15

"We got a Christmas card today from Dad and Pam." Nell looked up from her bowl. "Really? I didn't see it."

"I put it in the basket with the other cards," Felicity told her. "It's a picture of the three of them in Colorado. They went skiing there for a week in March."

Molly made a dismissive sound and put her spoon on the table next to her bowl. Nell had made a Portuguese style fish stew, but even the rich and savory dish couldn't tempt Molly to take more than a few bites.

"What do your friends think about you going to Switzerland next Christmas?" Nell asked Felicity.

"They think it's awesome, of course," Felicity said, ladling more stew into her bowl. "Except for Ricki. She hates the cold. She said if someone paid for her to go somewhere special for the holidays it would be a tropical island with plenty of sand and sun and fit guys in tiny bathing suits."

"Banana hammocks," Molly muttered.

Felicity laughed. "I bet Mick wouldn't be caught dead in one of those! Not that he has the time to be hanging out at the beach with all he has to do at the farm."

Molly suddenly rose from her seat. "I'm off," she said. "Mick and I are meeting some other members of the Young Farmer and Rancher Committee at the Blue Mermaid."

"What's with the long face?" Felicity asked. "You look like you're going to the dentist or something. It's just a bunch of people meeting in a pub."

"I'm sure these gatherings can get pretty heated," Nell said hurriedly.

Molly shot Nell a look of gratitude and was on her way.

"You know that bag I have my eye on?" Felicity asked. "This online store has it on sale. I sent you the link."

"Thanks," Nell said abstractedly.

"Do you want me to help clean up?"

"No," Nell said. "I'm sure you have more important things to do."

"Okay." Felicity took one last bite of stew, got up, and brought her bowl to the sink. "I'm going to call Dad. Should I say hi from you?" she asked.

Nell smiled. "Sure," she said. "Thanks."

When Felicity was gone, Nell's thoughts were finally free to turn again to Eric. Conversation at lunch had come easily for the most part. Eric hadn't mentioned their painful breakup or asked about her writing, for which Nell was grateful. He had suggested they see each other again, and she had assented. All of that was good.

Except for one thing, Nell realized, as she brought her empty bowl to the sink for rinsing. Here she was professing to be unhappy about her soon to be empty nest, and yet while her children were still with her, instead of focusing entirely on their well-being her thoughts were being tempted by the memory of a lost romance. *It's not my fault,* she thought defensively as she turned on the water. *It isn't.* It was just that Eric Manville's turning up in Yorktide this Christmas season was the last thing Nell had expected to happen. The absolute last. It was understandable that she should find herself to some extent preoccupied with him. It was understandable. Wasn't it?

It was almost midnight. The house was quiet but for the ticking of the miniature grandfather clock in the living room and the sound of the wind rattling the few old windows Nell was always meaning to replace. Softly she opened the door to her room and stepped into the hall. The doors of the girls' rooms were closed. Felicity was probably deep in sleep, but Molly might very well be staring into the darkness much as her mother had been doing since she had retired for the night.

Quietly, Nell began the journey she had decided upon only moments earlier. The attic of the house on Trinity Lane was accessed via a steep and narrow staircase hidden behind an equally narrow door at the end of the hall. The door creaked when she opened it, and Nell flinched. She reached for the pull cord, and a bare bulb overhead illuminated the stairs before her. Nell closed the door behind her—it creaked again—and, holding the banister, climbed the fourteen steps to the attic.

There she turned on another light that allowed her to see the center of the room if not every shadowy corner. Nell walked purposefully across the bare wooden boards to a plastic storage container labeled PRIVATE. There was a low stool nearby; Nell brought it closer and sat. She hadn't opened this container since she had packed it just after graduation from college. With a deep breath Nell snapped off the lid.

There they were, her old notebooks, and under them the journals in which her poetry had been published. The notebooks were five and a half by seven and a half inches and spiral bound. Nell had never written early drafts of her poems on a computer. She had felt the physical act of writing was in itself a part of the creating.

Nell lifted one of the notebooks from the plastic container and opened it. Immediately she recognized Eric's writing along with her own. She smiled as she remembered how she had so often asked for his input and how he had happily encouraged her process—*This works so well!*—and suggested changes—*Not sure about this word; try another?* She had never felt his contributions an intrusion or an attempted usurpation of her work. They had shared a sympathetic dialogue, a true give-and-take of ideas.

Nell took another notebook from the container and held it to her heart. These notebooks were all the tangible evidence that remained of her relationship with Eric. After the breakup she had packed into a separate box Eric's letters and the photos taken of them together and the trinkets and books he had given her and stored it in her parents' attic with the other boxes that contained memorabilia of her youth. When she married she had left that one special box where it was; to bring evidence of her earlier love affair into the home she was going to share with her husband seemed wrong. After the divorce Nell had been so occupied with the task of rebuilding a life she had virtually forgotten about the box, until three years earlier, when her parents had decided to sell their house and move to Florida. Nell had told her mother she would visit to pick up what remained of her belongings.

"Oh, I got rid of all that old junk that was littering up the attic," Jackie Emerson had said lightly. "That box from your college days weighed a ton. Your father almost threw his back out hauling it to the curb."

"But it was mine," Nell had replied, stunned and horrified. "That box contained *my* history. You had no right to deprive me of my past."

To which her mother had said, "Well, what's done is done."

Though there was much to be missed in that box, there was one photo in particular Nell would do anything to have in her possession. It had been taken at a picnic with friends one idyllic summer day. Nell could still hear the drowsy sound of bees buzzing; she could still smell the heady scent of roses; she could still feel the warmth of the sun on her skin and taste the tartness of the cold lemonade they had drunk. It had been a day of simple pleasures and deep happiness. She wondered if Eric remembered it as she did. Maybe, if things continued to go well between them, she would ask him. Maybe—

Nell shivered. The attic that could be so warm in the summer months was bone-shatteringly cold at this time of the year. She put the notebooks back into the plastic container and with some difficulty brought it down to her room, where she stowed it in her closet. Reading her old work would be an emotional experience and one Nell would have to approach carefully, but it was an experience she very much wanted. She removed her bathrobe, laid it across the end of her bed, and crawled under the covers. With the light turned out, Nell looked into the dark and remembered.

Chapter 16

Nell poured a second cup of coffee. Usually she drank only one in the morning, but she had been awake until almost two, haunted by memories of that long-lost summer day when she and Eric had been so simply and blissfully happy, so ignorant of the sadness and separation that was to come. Nell had been haunted, too, by thoughts of what happiness, however temporary, might be in store now that Eric had returned.

"Is that from Mick?" Nell asked, nodding at a gift bag from which red and green tissue paper stuck up like flames.

Felicity nodded. "I was up when he came by."

Molly suddenly appeared in the doorway, dressed in a cable-knit wool sweater over a pair of jeans. When she saw the gift bag on the table, she stopped in mid-stride.

Felicity held out the bag to her sister. "This is for you from Mick."

Reluctantly, it seemed to Nell, Molly continued toward the table and took the bag. "Did you say anything to him about Boston?" Molly asked, her tone urgent.

"Of course not. You asked me not to."

"Sorry." Molly reached into the bag and removed a little bundle wrapped in more tissue paper. Inside the bundle was a delicate painted glass ornament in the shape of a bird.

"A calling bird?" Nell guessed.

"Mick said he wasn't exactly sure what a calling bird was but he figured a songbird came close enough, and a nightingale is a songbird. Funny," Felicity added. "I always thought nightingales were really colorful, not mostly brown."

Nell looked closely at her older daughter, who still had not commented on the gift. "Molly?"

Molly shook her head quickly, as if to bring herself back to the moment. "It's nice," she said, wrapping the nightingale in the tissue paper and putting it back into the gift bag. Then she took her usual seat and poured a cup of coffee.

"Who was in the attic last night?" Felicity asked. "And don't say Santa Claus."

"Sorry," Nell said. "I was looking for something. Well, I'd better get a move on. Today is Mutts and Meows' annual open house." Nell kissed Molly's forehead on her way out of the kitchen. "You okay?" she asked softly.

Molly nodded.

"Eat something," Nell said. "You'll feel better."

As Nell was getting into her car a few minutes later, her mind preoccupied with Molly and her troubles, her phone alerted her to a text. It was from Eric. He wanted to know if she could meet at the end of her workday for a coffee. Without a moment's hesitation she sent him a text suggesting they meet at the Golden Apple again at three-fifteen. He agreed.

It was only when Nell was halfway to the clinic did she realize that all thoughts of her daughter had flown the moment she had seen Eric's text message. So much for being an attentive, devoted parent, Nell thought guiltily. *Keep a clear head,* she told herself, her hands tightening on the wheel. *Your children are your priorities. Not a relationship that ended in the long distant past.*

The Golden Apple was almost empty when Nell and Eric arrived within moments of each other. The aroma of freshly baked bread mingled with the sharp scent of freshly brewed coffee. "It smells like heaven in here," Eric noted as they took seats at a table. "Bread and coffee, two of life's greatest gifts."

"I agree, as would my daughters," Nell told him. "Molly has been drinking coffee since she was fifteen and Felicity could easily eat a loaf of bread a day."

When they had ordered, Nell asked how Eric's day had passed. "Busily," he replied, and he described a writing challenge with which he had been struggling. "You'd think that by now I'd know what I'm doing," he said, "but every so often a problem arises that makes me feel like a complete novice."

"What do you do when that happens?" Nell asked.

"Drink coffee," Eric said as the waitress delivered their orders. "And call my mother. She can usually talk me off a ledge."

"I should have asked after your parents before now," Nell said. "I hope they're well." Nell had met them only once, along with Eric's sister, Sarah, who had been about ten at the time. She remembered Mr. and Mrs. Manville as almost complete opposites of her own parents—warm, welcoming, and uncritical.

"They're great, thanks," Eric told her, handing Nell his phone. "That photo was taken this past summer in my parents' backyard. That's Chris, home on leave. Mom and Dad are on the right, Sarah is next to Dad, and those are my nephews. Peter's the ham and Luke's the one wearing the red t-shirt."

"Everyone looks very happy," Nell said, returning the phone to Eric. "And the boys are adorable."

"Sarah and Chris are doing a fine job. Peter and Luke are fantastic kids."

Nell smiled. "And you're a proud uncle."

"And the fun one. The kids are too young to understand that what I do is not really very important. All they know is that I'm occasionally on television and that the parents of their friends ask if they can get me to sign copies of my books. That makes Peter and Luke celebrities by proxy. Their father is the real hero, not me."

"They'll come to see that, I'm sure." Nell hesitated before going on. Only on the drive to the cafe had it struck her like a nasty blow that while not married, Eric might be romantically involved. True, he hadn't mentioned a girlfriend when they had talked about their marital status the day before when it might have been natural to do so. True, he had admitted he didn't have any particular reason to return home. But that didn't mean that he was single. If he was in a relationship, Nell thought, even if it was relatively new, she would not feel right about their spending time together. She had always had an unfashionably strict view of monogamy, a view it turned out that her former husband had not shared.

Before Nell could voice her question, Eric spoke. "I bet you're wondering if I'm in a relationship," he said. "The answer is I'm not. There's been no one since my divorce. And you?"

When Nell's head had ceased to whir—was Eric now a mind reader?—she answered his question. "There's been no one since my divorce, either," she told him. "These past six years I've been totally focused on making a good life for my daughters."

"But now your daughters are no longer—"

"Yes," Nell said quickly. She didn't want to hear the words spoken aloud. *Now they're no longer in need of so much care.*

Eric suddenly leaned forward and lowered his voice. "The man at the far table, the one wearing the buffalo plaid jacket. He's reading one of my early novels, *The Map of Our Lives.*"

Nell was glad for the radical change of topic. "I have a first edition of each of your books," she told him. "The owners of the Bookworm hold aside a copy for me. I had the same arrangement with the local bookstore back in Massachusetts."

"The beauty of the independent bookshop," Eric noted. "You know," he went on, "sometimes I still can't believe things have turned out as well as they have for me. No one ever thought I'd amount to much, and for so long I never gave anyone reason to think otherwise. My head was always in the proverbial clouds." Eric laughed. "It still pretty much is. I mean, look at what I do for a living. I earn money by telling tall tales."

"How did you find your talent as a novelist?" Nell asked. "I have to admit it's something I've often wondered about."

"It's an interesting story," Eric began. "I was twenty-three and working as a bagger at a grocery chain and basically at sixes and sevens—I always mean to look up the origins of that saying—and one day my neighbor happened to mention she was taking a weekend workshop in unlocking creativity. It sounded sufficiently vague and maybe even fun, and having nothing better to do that weekend, I signed up. When I got to the old campsite in the Berkshires, I found that one of the seminars was in the art of writing fairy tales. I'd never given any thought to an actual *person* writing a fairy tale. You know, all those stories your parents read to you when you're a kid seem somehow just *there*."

"Right," Nell said. "Part of what the world is and always was. Part of—forever."

"Exactly. I realized I wanted to find out what actually went on when a person sat down to create a fairy tale. I wanted to understand the power of fairy tales, what they could accomplish, why they were necessary. And that was the turning point."

"How do you mean?" Nell asked.

"Quite simply, it got me started writing. It was like a faucet had been switched on; stories just started coming, words just started flowing. Mostly awful stuff at first, but I stuck to it, read like crazy, wrote compulsively, until finally what I was writing was good. Then it was better." Eric smiled. "And then, through a series of fortunate events, I got my first book contract."

"At the tender age of thirty," Nell said.

"Yup. I'm very grateful for the nature of my talent."

Nell smiled. "Me too."

"So, do you read my books because you feel some sense of duty having known me back when?" Eric smiled. "Be honest."

"I read your work because I love it," Nell assured him. "Every new book pleases and enlightens me. And I've seen every movie made of your work. They're good, but I prefer the books to the films."

Eric laughed. "Me too. Besides I can't bear to go to openings. I mean, Hollywood? It's not me."

"You know, when your first book came out I was hesitant to read it," Nell admitted. "I wondered if I would find myself in one of the characters." *The cold-hearted destroyer of a gentle-hearted man.* "I know that's silly," Nell went on, "but I bet everyone who knows you has wondered at some point if he's going to show up on the page thinly veiled as the hero or the villain."

Eric nodded. "People I know are always seeking themselves in the characters I create, but the truth is that, while I might be inspired by a person's story, I'd never violate his or her privacy. That's not always a popular choice among writers, but it's what I'm comfortable with."

Before Nell could respond, Eric's phone rang and with an apology—"It's my publisher"—he answered. "Sure," he said after a moment. "That sounds fine. Just email me the details. Thanks. Merry Christmas to you, too."

"A book tour in the works," he explained. "They've got me going from coast to coast and everywhere in between."

"I haven't been farther away than New York City in years," Nell told him.

"Do you not like to travel?"

Nell didn't know how to answer. Why had it become so difficult for her to identify her likes and dislikes, her interests and passions? If her daughters made a gingerbread Pam, they could decorate the cookie with all sorts of symbols that represented their stepmother—skis; gold medals; expensive watches; flags from foreign nations. Pam displayed to the world a fully formed person, whereas she, Nell King, did not.

"I guess I've just been too busy to travel," she said finally. It wasn't true, but it was all she could find to say.

"I'd love to get together again," Eric said suddenly. "Maybe we could meet tomorrow, late afternoon? I need to spend a solid three or four hours on the book, and for some reason mornings are proving to be more productive than afternoons this time around."

Nell agreed to Eric's suggestion, and they left the café. No sooner had the door closed behind them than Eric's cell phone rang again. He looked at it and gave Nell an apologetic smile. "It's my agent," he said. "I should answer. She always takes my calls, no matter how busy she is."

"Of course," Nell said quickly. Eric nodded, took the call, and waved a farewell.

Nell got behind the wheel of her car, struggling against a feeling of letdown. She would be lying if she claimed she hadn't been looking forward to another hug. But that had been silly on her part. Most likely the emotional high of having come across each other after all the years apart had already dissipated for Eric. Of course it had. He had so many other aspects of his life on which to spend his time and energy, while she had . . . Nell didn't finish the thought.

Chapter 17

Nell had baked lasagna with ricotta cheese from a local supplier and tomato sauce she had made and frozen at the end of the season. Jill had eaten enough for two, somewhat making up in Nell's mind for Molly's lack of appetite. Jill didn't much enjoy cooking for one; Nell feared she wouldn't much enjoy it, either. Maybe once the girls were gone she could have Jill for dinner two or three nights a week . . . But that would be using her friend as a crutch, rather than making a true gesture of generosity.

"Hey, where were you before?" Felicity asked as she loaded the top basket of the dishwasher with glasses and small bowls. "I thought you'd be home right after work, but the house was empty when I got in from debate club."

"I had some errands to run," Nell said quickly.

Jill gave her a look that said "Liar, liar, pants on fire," and Nell turned back toward the sink.

Felicity looked toward the door of the kitchen and lowered her voice. "I've been thinking about what Mick is going to give Molly tomorrow. It's day five. Golden rings. Do you think he'll give her an engagement ring?"

Jill shot a questioning look at Nell, and Nell ever so

slightly shook her head. No, Felicity still didn't know that her sister was planning to leave Mick after the holidays.

"I have no idea," Nell said, fervently hoping not, though only weeks ago the idea would have delighted her. "But let's not speculate in front of your sister."

Footsteps in the hall announced Molly's return. She had changed into sweats and a flannel shirt, perfect for spending a few hours with the rambunctious eight-year-old Robinson twins. "I'm going to grab some coffee before I go," she said. "Is there any left in the pot?"

"Just enough for one cup, I think," Nell told her.

"I forgot to tell you guys that Pam sent me a link to the hotel where we'll be staying next year," Felicity announced. "It's amazing. It's got all these twinkling white lights hanging from the balconies like delicate branches. *So* pretty. And there's so much else to do besides ski. You can go horseback riding or get a massage or take a steam in the sauna. They have a tennis court and a library and a sun terrace. And there's a pool. And I'll have my own room, of course."

"Sounds like heaven," Molly remarked dryly, taking a sip of her coffee.

"The reality is usually not as perfect as the hype would lead you to believe," Jill pointed out.

Felicity frowned. "You guys are downers. Nothing's going to spoil my excitement about this trip."

Molly put her empty cup into the dishwasher and glanced at her watch. "I'm off," she said. "I won't be home until late. Mrs. Robinson said this holiday party she and her husband go to every year is pretty wild."

"It's a good thing you've got so many babysitting clients," Felicity said. "Rents in Boston are super expensive. That's what Dad says, anyway."

Molly made no response.

"Drive carefully," Nell said.

Molly promised and took her leave.

Felicity dried her hands on a dishtowel and tossed it onto the counter by the sink. "I'm off, too, but I won't be late. Robina has such a strict curfew it's ridiculous."

"You be careful, too," Nell said, closing the door of the dishwasher.

"Now that we're alone," Jill said when Felicity had gone, "I can ask how things went with Eric this afternoon."

"Fine."

"Just fine?" Jill pressed. "What did you talk about?"

"We mostly talked about his family and his work." Nell hesitated before going on. "He told me there's been no one romantic in his life since his divorce."

"And no one romantic in your life since yours. Did you tell him that?"

"Yes. He asked if we could get together again."

"And of course you said yes."

"Not of course," Nell said quickly. She didn't want to admit to Jill that she had been so absorbed in conversation with Eric that her daughters had temporarily become shadowy figures in the background of her consciousness. "I mean, there's no harm in having coffee with an old friend, is there?"

"There might be harm in just about anything," Jill noted. "If there *is* harm in seeing your long-lost love in the here and now, that's something for you to decide."

"Sometimes you're so maddeningly—" Nell broke off in frustration.

"Maddeningly what?" Jill asked.

Smart, Nell thought. "Nothing. Sorry. It's been a long day."

"Then I'll leave you to get some beauty rest. Good night, Nell. Thanks again for dinner."

When Jill too had gone, Nell was left alone in the kitchen

with her thoughts. If there *was* harm in her meeting with Eric, well, the damage had already been done, hadn't it? Still, it probably wasn't wise to see him again. Clearly he had a rich and busy life that had nothing to do with hers. The more often they got together, the more obvious the vast distance between them would become, and the more likely it would be for Eric to decide to cut short his visit to Yorktide before any more of his precious time was wasted.

Nell sighed, turned off the overhead light, and left the kitchen. No, it probably wasn't wise for her to meet with Eric again. But she knew without a doubt that she would.

Chapter 18

Nell and Molly were sitting at the kitchen table, the remains of breakfast before them. Well, the remains of Nell's breakfast. Molly had taken nothing but a cup of coffee laced with milk and sugar. She hadn't spoken, either, but to ask Nell if there was any errand she could run for her on the way home from classes. Nell had said there was not. The tension in the room was high.

When the doorbell rang, both women jumped in their seats. Nell looked at Molly, whose face had gone ashen. "Do you want me to get it?" she asked quietly.

Molly shook her head, slowly got up from the table, and left the room. Nell followed her as far as the little hall between the dining room and the living room, from where, if she kept close to the wall, she could hear and partially see what went on by the front door.

Mick had already come into the house. In the palm of her hand Molly was holding what was unmistakably a ring box. *Oh, no,* Nell thought. *Please not this.*

"Aren't you going to open it?" Mick asked. There was a mix of hope and fear in his voice, of excitement and just a little bit of dread.

Without a word, Molly lifted the hinged lid on the little box. Nell couldn't quite see the look on her daughter's face, though she didn't fail to notice the tense set of her shoulders.

"It's real gold," Mick said hurriedly. "It belonged to my grandmother. My grandfather gave it to her on their tenth wedding anniversary. They were too poor to afford a ring when they got married. She wore it until the day she died. Since she had no granddaughters she left it to me."

Nell swallowed hard. The implication was clear. Mick would give the ring to the woman he married.

"Oh." Molly managed a ghost of a smile.

"It's a promise ring," Mick went on. "I promise to love you forever. Here, let me put it on for you."

As Mick slipped the ring onto the fourth finger of Molly's right hand, Nell fought the urge to dash forward and put an end to the farce. *No,* she thought. *This is not a farce. This is the stuff of tragedy, and I have no rightful place in it.*

"Thank you," Molly said quietly. She did not return Mick's promise.

Mick didn't seem bothered or disappointed by her simple response. "We've got a plumber coming to the house this morning so I'd better be off." He leaned forward and kissed Molly on the cheek.

When Molly had closed the front door behind him, Nell came into the living room. Molly looked at her mother and laughed a bit wildly. "What's he going to give me for Christmas, a marriage license?"

"You accepted the ring," Nell stated. "Why?"

"I don't know. I . . . I didn't know what else to do!"

"You can't keep it," Nell said quietly. "Not if you're intending to break up with him. You don't have a right to it.

You have to be honest with him, Molly. It's not fair what you're doing."

"I know," Molly cried. "I know! It's just . . . I'm confused, Mom. Suddenly, I don't know what I want. Moving away . . . Mick . . . the farm . . . It's all so . . ."

"What's going on?" It was Felicity, thundering down the stairs. "Was Mick here? I thought I heard the doorbell but I was in the shower so I couldn't be sure."

Nell turned to her younger daughter. "Mick gave your sister a promise ring. It belonged to his grandmother."

Felicity squealed. "OMG, it's like you're engaged!" she cried. "Let me see it!"

"No," Molly said curtly. "It's not like I'm engaged. I've got to get to class."

She was gone before either her mother or her sister could say another word.

Felicity frowned. "What was that about? I thought she'd be thrilled. I mean it looks like Mick's going to propose soon, maybe on Christmas Day. That's probably the big surprise."

"I told you the other day," Nell said lamely. "Your sister is under a lot of strain at school. I think we just need to give her some space."

"I've never understood what that means, giving someone space. Is it like a polite way of ignoring someone? Well, whatever. I'm off to school." Felicity kissed her mother's cheek, grabbed her bag from the small table just inside the front door, and hurried out of the house.

Nell sighed. Her older daughter had always been a straightforward, even a transparent person, but now Nell felt sure that Molly was hiding something important, possibly even from herself. After all, she had admitted that she no longer knew what it was she really wanted. *I'm her mother*, Nell thought, her frustration mounting. *I should be able to help her understand what it is that she needs to be happy.*

Nell's cell phone rang, distracting her from her thoughts. It was Jill.

"Do you by any chance have dried mustard?" Jill asked. "I'm feeling too lazy to drive into town."

"Sorry," Nell said. "It's not something I usually have around."

"It was worth a try. By the way, I haven't heard from Stuart in weeks. Usually we've made a plan for Christmas dinner by now."

"Our children are keeping us on our toes this season," Nell commented.

"As in Molly and her plan to run away?"

"I'm not sure she would call it running away," Nell said, "but yes. And guess what just happened. Mick gave her his grandmother's wedding ring as a promise to love her forever, and she accepted it. To be exact, she didn't protest his putting it on her finger."

"Almost as bad as an engagement ring," Jill said. "Well, you know what I mean. What's she going to do?"

Nell sighed. "Your guess is as good as mine. I just hope she speaks up soon. The longer she keeps silent about her intentions, the more damage she's doing to Mick and to her own peace of mind."

"Agreed," Jill said. "But remember, this is Molly's life, not yours. Try not to let her woes overwhelm you."

"I'll try," Nell promised, and they ended the call.

With the girls gone and her phone back in her pocket, the house suddenly felt very empty. The silence was thundering, and into that thundering silence came the call of the old notebooks and journals stashed in Nell's bedroom closet. Again she realized that at some point before Eric left town he might ask about her poetry. Nell had no idea how he would react to the news that she hadn't written a word in more than twenty years. Possibly the information wouldn't affect him in the least. And maybe he wouldn't ask in the first place, having long ago ceased to be invested in the girl who broke his heart. But if that were true, why did Eric want to see her again?

Nell rubbed her forehead. Eric Manville. The temptation of poetry. The joys and sorrows of the past, both before and during her marriage. They were all dragging her attention away from what was *really* important. Making this Christmas, possibly their last together as a family of three, perfect for her children.

The stockings, Nell thought, heading upstairs to her bedroom. *I'll work on the girls' Christmas stockings.*

Nell was dusting the furniture in the living room later that day—not easy to do what with the Christmas decorations on every available surface—when her cell phone rang. It was Eric.

"Hi," she said brightly. Her earlier anxiety had largely eased away, thanks to the soporific effects of daily routine and, more specifically, of housework. A tidy house allows for a tidy mind. It was something her mother always used to say.

"Hi," Eric said. "Nell, I'm afraid I'm going to have to cancel our get-together this afternoon. I'm sorry."

"Oh." The dust cloth fell from Nell's hand to the floor and she bent over to retrieve it. "Sure," she said. "No problem."

"I just got a call from my friend Hal," Eric went on. "He owns a fantastic little bookstore in Cambridge. When I told him I was in Ogunquit, he asked if I could possibly come to a holiday open house this evening to mingle and sign a few books. I felt I couldn't say no. Hal has come through for my family and me more times than I can count. He gave Sarah a job all through college."

"Of course," Nell said with a heroic attempt at sounding neutral and unmoved. "It's the right thing to do."

"Thanks, Nell. I knew you'd understand. I'll let you know when I get back tonight, okay?"

Nell struggled to find her voice over the lump that was building in her throat. "Sure," she said finally. "Bye."

Nell stuck the phone back into her pocket. She felt keenly disappointed, though she knew she had no right to be. Eric didn't owe her anything, not after all this time. *Face it,* Nell thought, and not for the first time. *He means a lot to me but I just don't mean that much to him.* Before the reading at the Bookworm Jill had suggested that Nell ask herself just what it was she wanted from seeing Eric Manville after a separation of more than twenty years. *But I didn't take that advice to heart,* Nell thought. *I didn't prepare to . . . to be disappointed.*

Dust cloth in hand, Nell went to the kitchen where Molly was sitting at the table with a textbook opened before her. She was still wearing the ring Mick had given her that morning. Turning toward the fridge Nell noticed that two windows on the Advent Calendar hadn't yet been opened. She was surprised she hadn't noticed before now.

"Why haven't you or your sister opened the windows for the seventeenth and eighteenth?" she asked.

Molly looked up from her textbook and shrugged. "I forgot. Fliss probably did, too."

"Why don't you open the windows now?" Nell suggested.

"That's okay," Molly said. "You can do it."

Nell shook her head. "But I bought the calendar for you girls."

"Mom." Molly sighed. "We're not little kids. We don't care about stuff like that."

"Like what?" Nell was aware of the tone of hurt in her voice. She hadn't meant her feelings to be so plain, but she felt so raw at the moment, raw and vulnerable.

"Like Advent calendars and matching aprons. That stuff is okay when you're a kid, but . . ." Molly suddenly got up from the table. "Okay, Mom. If it makes you happy I'll open the windows."

Nell watched as her older daughter dutifully opened the two windows on the calendar and realized that she *didn't* feel particularly happy about it. "I was thinking of making that meatloaf you and Felicity like so much for dinner," she said.

Molly went back to the table and her textbook. "Sure, Mom," she said. "Whatever."

Chapter 19

Nell had indeed made the meatloaf she had mentioned earlier to Molly, and though it was highly flavored with black pepper and oregano, Nell found that she barely tasted it. It was unlike her to eat mechanically. It was also unlike her to be checking her phone for incoming calls or texts while at the table, but that was exactly what she was doing. She hadn't entirely convinced herself that Eric wouldn't call that night upon his return from Cambridge.

"Guess what Ella's father is giving her mother for Christmas," Felicity said. "A brand-new Jaguar. Can you believe it? It's a total surprise. I mean, Ella knows but her mother doesn't have a clue."

"They must have a lot of money to throw around," Molly said with a frown of disapproval.

"I wouldn't call buying a car throwing money around," Felicity protested.

"I would, especially when it's a totally impractical car to have in Maine. She won't be able to drive it for half of the year."

"Mom?" Felicity asked. "What do you think?"

Nell looked up from her phone. "Sorry, what did you say?" she asked.

Felicity frowned. "Who are you expecting to hear from, Mom?"

"No one," Nell lied.

"Then why do you keep checking your phone?" Molly asked.

Nell slipped the phone into the pocket of her sweater. She felt a bit chastened. How many times had she asked her daughters not to use the phone during a meal? And here she was, behaving like a lovestruck teen waiting to hear from her crush.

"So, what do you think of Ella's father buying Ella's mother a Jaguar for Christmas? Do you think it's a silly purchase?"

"I think it's none of our business how other people spend their money," Nell replied.

"I wonder what Dad's getting Pam," Felicity mused.

Molly rolled her eyes, and though Nell resisted that particular urge she, too, had no desire to entertain the question. Silence descended on the table, and as Nell poked at her meal she was struck by a sudden surge of annoyance that bordered on anger. Why did Eric have to breeze back into her life at just this time only to highlight her feelings of loss and inadequacy? Why had she gone to that reading in the first place? And to think she had been foolish enough to consider asking Eric if he remembered the summer day on which that long-lost photo had been taken! Reconnecting with Eric was getting her absolutely nowhere and would only result in—

"Ugh!" Felicity cried. "It feels like I'm sitting here with Scrooge and the Grinch! Why are you two so unhappy and distracted and grumpy?"

"Sorry," Nell said automatically.

Molly got up from the table and brought her dishes to the sink. "I've got a lab report to write," she said. "Thanks for dinner, Mom."

"Let's watch *A Charlie Brown Christmas* after dinner," Nell suggested when Molly was gone. "Or we could make popcorn balls. I found a super easy recipe online earlier."

"That's okay," Felicity said. "If Ella is around, I'll drive over to her place for a bit." Felicity took her phone from her pocket and began to text her friend.

Nell stabbed at the remains of the meatloaf on her plate. She wondered if at that very moment Eric was chatting with an adoring female fan. He had become a media darling after the success of his first book, and the truth was that he was kind and good and smart and any woman in her right mind would welcome the chance to know him and to possess more of him than a grainy photo from the local newspaper.

"See you later, Mom." Felicity was getting up from her chair. "I'm going to Ella's house."

"Okay," Nell said. "Drive safely."

"You always say that."

"And," Nell replied, "I always mean it."

The curtains were closed against the night, but a sliver of moonlight had made its way into Nell's room. She was tucked up in bed with one of her old notebooks and a biography of William Blake she had first read in college. The author of *Songs of Experience and Songs of Innocence* had always fascinated her. Slowly she paged through the sections of the fantastical color illustrations—The Raising of Lazarus, Jacob's Dream, the wildly famous portrait of

Newton—and found that lines from "The Tyger" were running through her mind. ". . . *In what distant deeps or skies/Burnt the fire of thine eyes?/On what wings dare he aspire/What the hand, dare seize the fire?*"

William Blake would probably not have appreciated cell phones, Nell thought as hers rang loudly in the quiet of the room. She reached for it on the bed beside her. It was Eric. "Hi," she said with a sense of palpable relief.

"You sound surprised. I told you I'd call when I got back from Cambridge. Is it too late? Did I wake you?"

"No," Nell assured him, putting the book aside. "It's not too late. How was the event?"

"Mobbed. It was a lot of fun and a big success for Hal, I think."

Nell experienced a twinge of jealousy, of which she felt immediately ashamed. Of what was she jealous? Eric's popularity? His wealth? His many friendships? Nell glanced at the old notebook by her side and felt keenly her own lack of ambition. She had taken no steps in her life to win such prizes, and there was no one to blame but herself.

"I'm glad you had a good time," she managed to say.

"How was your afternoon?" he asked.

"It was fine."

"And the girls? How are they?"

"They're fine, too," she said. "Getting ready for finals. Spending time with their friends. Dropping hints about what they want for Christmas. Well, Felicity is. Molly's not much of a materialist."

"Hey, apropos of nothing," Eric said, "guess what I was thinking about on the drive back tonight? The day we rode the swan boats in the Public Gardens and one of the swans, the real ones I mean, came charging at us. One of us screamed—it might have been me—and the kid manning the pedals dove into the water, leaving us stranded."

Nell laughed. "How could I forget? Luckily the swan lost interest in us. They can be pretty vicious when they're protecting their young."

"I hadn't thought of that incident in ages," Eric admitted. "It's funny, but suddenly the years we were together seem so close."

"Yes," Nell said, glancing again at the old notebook in which both she and Eric had written out their thoughts and feelings. "They do. And yet . . . and yet they also seem so very far away."

"Yes," Eric replied softly. "I know what you mean. Well, I should let you get some sleep. Good night, Nell."

"Good night, Eric."

Nell plugged her phone into its charger. She was very pleased that Eric had phoned and recalled with a bit of surprise the moments since they had last met when she had rued her decision to attend the reading at the Bookworm. Suddenly Nell remembered another afternoon when she and Eric had been in the Public Gardens. A fierce rainstorm had broken out with little warning. Hand in hand they had ducked under a massive oak tree, where they had kissed passionately and shamelessly as only the young can do in full view of the world. Only when the storm had long passed did they emerge from under the protection of the branches, aglow with happiness.

Nell put a hand to her chest. Their romance had been so very passionate. Of course, it was true that intense passion never lasted for very long. If she and Eric had stayed together, one day the strength of their physical desire for each other would have weakened. No, Nell decided now, tucked in her bed on Trinity Lane. It would not have weakened. It would have transmuted into something more mellow but just as strong and wonderful. She thought of what Eric had said about the shiny gold ring becoming lovelier over time as it was marked by experience, both good and bad.

It was a beautiful image and one to treasure.

Chapter 20

Ever since she was a girl Nell had gotten a kick out of the police blotter page in the local paper. This morning, the nineteenth of December, she learned that the guy who owned the Flipper had run a red light; that a twelve-year-old girl had been caught shoplifting a box of Hostess cupcakes at the convenience store; and that a local artist who went by the name of Nico had called the police to report a possible intruder that turned out to be his neighbor's cat. Nell smiled. Running a red light, shoplifting, and breaking into someone's home (if you were a human) might be wrong, but they were hardly the stuff of big-city crime. Life in Yorktide was pretty darn good.

Nell turned the page, and her eye was caught by an advertisement for a poetry course being offered at the community college. The course was geared for those with some academic background in poetry. The cost was reasonable, and the class would conveniently meet every Monday evening for six weeks starting in early January. It all sounded too good to be true. Nell reached for her phone to sign up online and then hesitated. When she had been reading and writing poetry seriously she had been so much more self-aware, so much more *alive* than she had been since succumbing to her parents' pressure to end things with Eric, an act that had led to her abandoning her other great passion. Nell just wasn't sure she had what it would take to return to poetry. Not quite yet. Not until she tested the waters further.

With a sense of determination Nell got up from the table, went into the living room, and stood before the floor-to-ceiling built-in bookcases that stood at right angles to each other, creating a sort of book nook. Two shelves were packed with books Nell had collected in high school and college. There were several hefty Norton anthologies; collections of the work of poets she had binge read back before binging on anything but food was a thing, poets such as Emily Dickinson and John Donne, Frank O'Hara and Anne Sexton. There were volumes of poetry she had read in translation, like the work of Adam Zagajewski and Charles Baudelaire, as well as slim, self-published works by other young poetry students in whose company Nell had spent so much of her youth.

Nell removed several of the books from the shelves and settled into one of the comfortable armchairs nearby. All but one volume she stacked on the carpet at her feet. The volume she kept at hand was a collection of the poems of Wallace Stevens. Nell opened at random to find one of Stevens's most well known works, "The Emperor of Ice Cream."

Before she could read the first line, the girls came down the stairs one after the other. When they saw their mother in the book nook they halted.

"What's up?" Molly asked curiously. "I haven't seen you sit down to read in ages. Maybe ever."

"You might need to get used to it," Nell told them. "I've decided to get back to reading poetry. I used to live and breathe poetry. I wrote poems as well."

"I never knew that," Felicity said, sinking into the armchair across from Nell's.

There's so much about me you don't know, Nell thought. *That no one knows. No one but Eric.*

"Did Dad know?" Molly asked, picking up a copy of Shakespeare's sonnets from the stack of books at her mother's feet. "He's not exactly a serious literature kind of guy."

"He knew that I used to write," Nell told her, "but honestly, I don't think it much registered with him."

"Why did you stop writing poetry when you liked it so much?" Felicity asked.

Nell closed the volume of Stevens's poems. "It's hard to explain," she said. "I found that once I was married I couldn't . . . I guess I couldn't concentrate." *Couldn't,* she added silently, *or wouldn't? I wouldn't give my work the attention it deserved. I wouldn't give myself the attention I deserved.*

"That's too bad," Felicity said. "Were you published?"

"Yes. A few of my poems were published in my college's poetry journal and a few were published in literary journals with a wider readership. One of my professors encouraged me to apply to a prestigious graduate program but . . . but in the end I didn't."

"Because you were marrying Dad?" Molly asked, looking up from the book of sonnets with a frown.

"That was only partly why," Nell said. *The other part,* she added silently, *was because I was afraid and unsure.*

"Can we read some of your stuff?" Felicity asked. "Not that I know much about poetry. I like Robert Frost, though, especially 'Stopping by Woods on a Snowy Evening.'"

"Maybe some day." Nell gestured to the books on the floor. "This all is . . . Well, it's bringing up a lot of memories."

"What kind of memories?" Molly asked, putting the volume of sonnets back on the stack.

"Bittersweet." *Memories of Eric and me,* Nell thought. *Memories of a time when options seemed limitless and the future seemed rosy.*

"Why now, Mom?" Felicity asked. "Why are you suddenly interested in poetry again?"

"I don't know exactly," Nell prevaricated. "A whim I guess."

"Whims come from somewhere," Molly said quietly.

Felicity got up from her chair. "So what are you baking today, Mom?"

The question took Nell by surprise. "I haven't thought about it yet. I'll whip up something."

"Or you could take the day off," Felicity suggested. "We've still got about a pound of oatmeal raisin cookies and about six pounds of peanut butter bars. Slight exaggeration."

Nell smiled. "I'll consider taking a break." Then she turned to Molly. "Has Mick come by yet?" she asked.

"First thing. Six geese a-laying. He brought a dozen goose eggs."

Felicity laughed. "At least he's not bringing you real birds! I'm going to grab one of those peanut butter bars and be off. See you guys later."

"I'll make a quiche with the eggs tonight if you'd like," Nell offered when Felicity had gone.

"I don't really care what happens to the eggs," Molly said roughly. "I'm half tempted to break them down the kitchen sink."

"Molly." Nell sighed. "You need to talk to him."

"I can't, Mom. I just can't. Not yet. I'll see you later. I'm meeting Andrea at the library."

When Molly had gone, Nell again opened the volume of Wallace Stevens's poetry. "The Anecdote of the Jar." Not an easy work to fathom. For a moment her eyes swept over the lines and her brain refused to focus. And then, quite suddenly, something changed and Nell began to read and to listen and to experience the poem in the way she once had so long ago.

When she had read through the poem three times Nell realized that she was crying. She smiled. *I've done it,* she thought. *I've done it.*

"Is there anything about this part of Maine that isn't charming?" Eric asked. "This cafe, this road . . . Everything just feels so, well, charming."

Nell smiled. "Even mud season has its moments, like when you spot the first brave little yellow crocus that's popped up in the far corner of your garden."

They were meeting at another family-owned café on a quiet little road in Kennebunk. Directly across from the Butter Churn was a cemetery with graves dating back to the seventeenth century. Like similar cemeteries throughout New England it had a strangely comforting appeal for Nell, who found the efforts of the living to memorialize their loved ones gone ahead deeply moving. Old cemeteries reinforced her belief in love and kindness.

Though the café was toasty thanks to a wood-burning stove in one corner, Eric kept his puffer coat on and his scarf wrapped around his neck and revealed a pair of fingerless gloves under a pair of battered suede mittens. "Funny thing is," he said, as a waitress brought their coffees to the table, "I actually like the cold, even though I feel it so acutely."

"I know," Nell told him. "I remember when a bunch of us built a snowman in front of the science building. You were as excited as a little kid. When the rest of us felt frostbitten and decided to quit, you declared you'd finish the snowman on your own. And you did."

"That was a wonderful day, wasn't it?"

"Yes," Nell said. "It was."

Eric took a sip of his coffee and carefully placed the mug back on the table. "We haven't talked about the elephant in the room," he said quietly.

Nell's heart began to race and she folded her hands to steady them. "Oh," she said.

Eric leaned forward across the small round table. "It's just that I've always wondered . . . Well, I guess I never entirely believed the reason you gave for ending our relationship."

Nell looked into his dear and familiar eyes. "You were right not to believe me when I told you I didn't love you anymore," she said. "It was a lie, one I'd half convinced myself to believe. I'm not proud of my behavior. I bought into my parents' opinion that I needed protection. I bought into their message about what marriage should be for a young woman. Safety. Security. Stability." Nell shook her head. "You'd think I was a sheltered Victorian maiden the way they went on. And yet, I listened."

Eric sighed. "I had a feeling your parents were behind it. Of course they wouldn't have regarded me as a good bet for safety or security or stability."

"But why should it have been your job to take care of me as if I had no will of my own?" Nell asked. "Why should you have been anyone other than who you were?

And that should have been enough for me. I never believed in you the way I should have. I did you a grave disservice assuming that you would fail us both. I'm sorry."

Eric smiled kindly. "I'm glad I finally know the truth."

"And look where turning against my own instincts and being a dutiful daughter got me," Nell said ruefully. "Left for a younger woman, one child refusing to have anything to do with her father, the other worshipping the ground he walks on. And both daughters desperate to get away from good old mom."

"Desperate?" Eric asked with a smile. "Really?"

"Maybe I'm exaggerating," Nell admitted. "In reality they just want to move on with their lives."

"Then you've done your job as a parent."

"There should be some consolation in that, I suppose."

"Were you in love with Joel?" Eric asked suddenly. "I know it's a pushy question."

"That's all right," Nell said. "No, I was never in love with him, but I did care for him. After the initial shock of his leaving wore off, sure, I felt angry and humiliated, but honestly, not for very long. The divorce didn't break me as it might have had I really loved Joel." Nell paused. "Mostly I loved my big house and my sure status in the community. I loved that my parents were proud of me. I loved my nice clothes and my swimming pool and my ridiculously expensive hair stylist. I loved that things like plumbing problems and electric bills were taken care of without my having to lift a finger." Nell shuddered. "I find it hard to believe I could have been so . . . so shallow."

Eric put his hands over hers, still folded on the table before her. "The Nell I know could never be shallow. We all seek comfort and security. Sometimes we make mistakes in our pursuit of both. That's all."

The feel of Eric's hands embracing hers made Nell feel something she hadn't felt since long before the divorce: comforted. "Then maybe the word is *afraid*," she said finally.

"Being afraid is not a crime or a sin," Eric countered. "Sometimes it's even the smart thing to be. The world can be a scary place."

"You're being too nice to me. But thank you."

"So, you *did* love me at the end?" Eric asked softly.

"Yes," Nell said. "I lied to the both of us when I said that I didn't and walked away. I lied to myself when I decided to marry Joel. The up and coming man, as my father used to say."

"I want to ask another pushy question," Eric said, letting go of her hands and sitting back in his chair. "What about your writing? I'm kind of surprised you haven't mentioned it."

Nell laughed a bit awkwardly. "I've been hoping you wouldn't ask," she admitted.

Eric frowned. "Why?"

"Because I haven't written a word of poetry in more than twenty years."

"I'm sorry to hear that," Eric said promptly. "I've kept an eye out for your name in poetry circles. I assumed I missed it because there are so many fairly obscure publications out there. What happened, Nell?"

"I'll try to explain. Do you remember Professor Ferrari?" she asked.

"Your biggest fan next to me. She was a fantastic teacher. She urged you to apply for that prestigious graduate program at the University of Chicago."

"She did, and she was so disappointed when I told her I wasn't going on to graduate school. She asked me why, and I just babbled a bunch of lame excuses. The truth was that I was scared of failing—and of achieving, though that part didn't dawn on me until much, much later. My parents said they wouldn't pay for grad school, and the thought of somehow managing it on my own didn't seem possible. Add to that the fact that I'd ended our relationship and I suddenly realized I was totally unsupported." Nell sighed. "And then I started to date Joel and the next thing I knew we were married and I'd had the children and there didn't seem to be time or space for . . . for me. At least I didn't allow there to be."

"I'm sorry," Eric said. "Really sorry. But surely things can be different now. What's to stop you from being open to inspiration?"

Nell finally took a sip of her coffee, now almost cold. "You can't compel the Muse to take up residence," she said.

"No, but you can adopt an attitude of receptivity."

"Yes," Nell agreed. "After we met the other day I dug out my old notebooks. I remembered what it was like to read to you my work in progress. I remembered what it was like to talk with you about what I was trying to achieve."

"The remembering sounds like a step toward writing," Eric noted.

"I'm not so sure I *can* write again," Nell said. "It might be enough that I relearn how to read poetry seriously and joyfully."

"And have you begun that journey?"

"I've very barely begun," Nell told him. "We'll see if I get on."

"Why wouldn't you get on, if it's something you really want to do?"

Nell laughed, though she didn't find the question at all amusing. "Laziness?" she suggested. "A lack of belief in my ability to see and hear and understand?"

"It sounds as if you're deliberately putting stumbling blocks in your way." Eric leaned forward again. "I'm sorry. I don't mean to make you angry. But I do mean to provoke you, because I believe in you, Nell."

Nell shook her head. "Why? What have I done to earn your belief in me?"

"You don't have to earn my belief in you. It's just *there*. It always has been." Eric smiled. "Don't ask me to explain why I feel what I feel. It's hard enough to get my characters to explain themselves to the reader—and to me."

"Novels are odd things, aren't they?" Nell said with a laugh.

"Tell me about it."

"My coffee is cold."

"Mine's gone. Maybe we should head out," Eric suggested. "There's a chapter that's giving me serious grief. I'm hoping to wrestle it into some sort of shape before tomorrow."

When they had paid and left the café, Eric reached for Nell and embraced her.

"Thank you for being honest with me about what happened between us," he said softly before releasing her.

Nell looked into his beautiful, soulful eyes. "The least I owe you is honesty."

"See you again?"

"Yes," Nell said. "Of course."

Nell watched as Eric walked to his car. When he had gotten behind the wheel she slid into her own car and breathed a huge sigh of relief. The secrets had been told; the air had been cleared; the lies had been exposed. And Eric hadn't walked away in disgust when she had admitted her weaknesses. Instead he had told her that he believed in her.

Someone still *believed* in her.

Chapter 21

Everyone seemed to have enjoyed the swordfish Nell had made for dinner, even Molly, though Nell was loath to read anything into her daughter's sudden return of appetite.

"Where were you this afternoon, Mom?" Felicity asked. "And don't tell me you were buying more tinsel, because we have enough to last ten lifetimes."

Nell shot a glance at Jill, who was studiously avoiding eye contact with her friend.

"I had some errands to run," she said as she brought the coffeepot to the table.

"Guess what Mick brought around today?" Felicity asked Jill.

"Six geese a-laying?" Jill said.

"A dozen goose eggs. They take up way less room than actual geese!"

"Though they are a good deal larger than the average chicken egg. Does Mick's family raise geese?" Jill asked Molly.

Molly shook her head. "No. He must have bought them from another farm."

"A lot of farmers barter their produce," Felicity pointed out. "Maybe Mick traded for the eggs. You should ask him, Molly."

"Why?" Molly asked testily. "What does it matter?"

"And now for dessert," Nell said quickly, hoping to avert the continuation of a conversation that was clearly approaching dangerous territory. She placed a dish in the middle of the table. "It's Montelimar-style white nougat. It's made with almonds, honey, vanilla, pistachios, brandy, and sugar."

"It's beautiful," Jill commented. "It looks like a gorgeous outcropping of rock."

"Less hard, I hope," Molly said with the ghost of a smile. "We don't have dental insurance."

"I just remembered something," Jill said. "When Stuart was little there was a bakery in South Berwick that sold gingerbread cookies with a paper image of Old Saint Nick pasted down on the icing. It was almost impossible to peel the paper completely off. You always wound up ingesting little shreds of Santa. One year Stuart couldn't be bothered with trying to get the paper off, so he ate the whole thing."

"Ugh," Felicity cried. "Did he get sick?"

"No. I was a bit freaked when I realized what he'd done, but he seemed fine, so . . ." Jill shrugged. "Little kids are fairly indestructible when you think about it."

"Christmas when Molly and Fliss were little was wonderful," Nell said. "I only regret that—"

"Here we go," Felicity interrupted with a laugh. "Mom's going to moan about how she's the only mother of everyone she knows who doesn't have a picture of her kids on Santa's lap!"

"I've got one," Jill said. "It's not a very good picture. The guy playing Santa had the most ludicrous looking fake beard I'd ever seen and Stuart was scared stiff of him.

Today I'd probably get in trouble for endangering the welfare of a child by forcing him to sit on some stranger's lap."

"So when are you going to Connecticut to see Stuart?" Felicity asked.

Jill shrugged. "He's been radio silent about plans."

"Maybe he's really busy at work."

"Stuart is never busy at work," Jill said dryly. "It's one of the reasons he keeps getting fired."

"Well, he can't have forgotten Christmas is only a few days from now," Felicity pointed out. "It's impossible to ignore the ads and the decorations and the music."

"Even when you wish you could ignore it all." Molly shrugged. "Sorry. Just not feeling very jolly at the moment."

"Well," Felicity said, "you've got Mick's next gift to look forward to. Seven swans a-swimming. Maybe that will put you in the holiday spirit."

"I doubt it," Molly said tersely.

Jill cleared her throat and studied her coffee. Nell opened her mouth to speak and closed it again.

"Is there something going on here?" Felicity demanded. "Is someone keeping a secret from me?"

"Of course not," Nell said quickly, reaching for a knife. "So, who wants a piece of nougat?"

Chapter 22

Felicity had left for school before seven. Nell and Molly were seated at the kitchen table. There were dark circles under Molly's eyes, as if she hadn't slept more than a moment during the night.

"You're not eating," Nell said.

Molly put down the spoon with which she had been toying with her oatmeal. "My stomach is in a knot."

"I can guess why. Molly—"

"Don't say anything, *please* Mom. Just don't."

"All right." Nell sighed. If only she could wave a magic wand or—

The doorbell rang, and Molly flinched.

"Do you want me to get it?" Nell asked.

"No." Molly got up from the table and left the kitchen.

For a brief moment Nell debated the rightness of following her daughter to witness the encounter with Mick, but she was already guilty of eavesdropping on the two. *It's a bit late for scruples,* she thought, pushing back her chair and moving quietly into the little hall between the dining and living room.

Mick was wearing a red wool beanie and his ubiquitous

Carhartt jacket. By his feet there was a mound of crumpled tissue paper. Molly was holding a large rectangular board.

"I found it at that antique place out by the Gascoyne farm," Mick was saying. "I couldn't believe my luck when I counted and realized there were exactly seven swans in the picture."

Molly continued to stare at the print. Suddenly, she thrust it toward Mick. "Stop it!" she cried. "Stop being so nice to me!"

Nell put her hand to her mouth. *Oh, Molly,* she thought. *Be careful . . .*

"Why shouldn't I be nice to you?" Mick asked with a bit of a nervous laugh. "What are you talking about?"

Nell watched as Molly's expression underwent a rapid and violent change from distress to cold resolve. "Because I have to break up with you," she said forcefully.

"What?" Mick shook his head; Nell could only imagine the look of confusion and dismay on his face. "Why?" he asked. "What did I do wrong?"

"You didn't do anything wrong. It's just that . . . It's just that I don't love you anymore, and you have to stop giving me things."

Nell winced. For all of Molly's earlier bravado, when face-to-face with Mick she was acting like an emotionally charged child. And Nell was painfully aware that she had behaved similarly when she had broken up with Eric all those years ago. She had lied to him. It had been a lie born of fear, as she suspected Molly's lie was as well. The past was playing itself out again, only this time Nell was a horrified witness rather than a cowardly participant.

Mick took a step closer to Molly. "I don't understand," he said. "What are you saying?"

Molly moved away. "I'm saying that I don't love you anymore. Please Mick, just . . . just go."

Nell held her breath in anticipation of Mick's protest, but there was none. Instead, he walked rapidly to the front door and left the house.

Quietly, Nell walked into the living room. "Do you want to talk about what just happened?" she asked her daughter.

Molly, who had been standing utterly still since Mick's departure, shook her head, tossed the print Mick had given her onto the couch, and ran up the stairs. Nell took a step to follow but decided not to. Instead, she retrieved the print from the couch. It was a lovely picture of a magnificent swan and her six cygnets on a calm blue lake surrounded by a smooth green lawn. The mat in which the print was framed was snowy white. Nell sighed and leaned it against the wall behind the Christmas tree where it would be safe.

Just before four o'clock that afternoon, Nell opened the front door to find Jill standing on the welcome mat that read: MERRY CHRISTMAS TO ALL WHO ENTER HERE! She was wrapped in the massive cream-colored wool cardigan she had brought back from a vacation in Ireland thirty years before. Jill claimed it was warmer than any coat she had ever owned.

"Hey," Nell said. "Come in. I'm just about to take a batch of raspberry thumbprints out of the oven."

"Wow," Jill said, removing her sweater as they entered the kitchen. "They smell beyond good."

"They should. I won't even tell you how much butter the recipe called for. And the raspberry jam is homemade by Margaret O'Connell, the woman who sells in pretty much every specialty food shop between here and Portland."

"The woman knows her jams and jellies. And her breads aren't bad, either. Have you had her Irish soda bread? Killer."

Nell opened the oven, carefully removed the tray of cookies, and set it on top of the stove. "So," she said, "what brings you by?"

Jill leaned against the counter and crossed her arms over her chest. "Stuart phoned me earlier. He's decided to spend Christmas in the Caribbean with his girlfriend of the moment. Which means I won't be going to Connecticut. I didn't argue. He's forty-four years old. He's his own man."

"I'm sorry, Jill," Nell said feelingly. "You must be disappointed, especially with this being the first year without Brian."

"I am disappointed," Jill admitted, "but I'm not entirely surprised. Stuart's failed me before. You can say a lot for nurture, but nature has something to do with the way a person turns out. And in too many ways Stuart displays aspects of his father's faulty character. I can't tell you how many jobs Stuart has lost due to insubordination or sheer laziness. And as for his romantic relationships . . ." Jill shook her head. "Stuart never met his father, but he's unmistakably his son."

"And you love him."

"Of course," Jill said. "I might not be particularly proud of how he's living his life, but that doesn't mean I won't go medieval on someone who tries to hurt him."

Nell laughed. "I know exactly what you mean."

"Still, it's hard not to blame yourself when your kid doesn't turn out exactly as you'd hoped he might," Jill said. "Every time Stuart breaks up with a girlfriend I think, why didn't I provide him with a solid male role model? And every time he loses a job I think, why didn't I teach him a better work ethic?"

"But each person is an autonomous individual," Nell pointed out, carefully sliding the cookies onto a cooling rack. "A parent can't be blamed for every poor decision an adult child makes."

Jill sighed. "Of course not. Still, being a parent puts you in a very strange place. Even when you don't much like your kid, you love him."

"Though there have to be exceptions to that. Some people must stop loving their children, for reasons they feel are legitimate."

Jill shuddered. "Probably, but I'd rather not think about that sort of thing. Christmas is supposed to be a time of peace, love, and understanding. I want to fill my head with visions of sugarplums, whatever they are, and not with thoughts of family strife."

"I agree. You know, I've been remembering so much about Christmases past this season. The good memories are simply flooding my consciousness."

"Share some of the good memories," Jill requested. "Distract me from my woes."

"Okay," Nell said. "For one, I keep thinking about the years when the girls were small. Christmas mornings were Norman Rockwell perfect, the girls in their flannel pajamas, Joel wearing one of his fine wool bathrobes, me in one of the silk robes he liked me to wear. The girls would literally squeal with excitement as they tore the wrapping paper off their presents. It was idyllic."

Jill raised an eyebrow. "How much are you romanticizing the past?"

"I don't think that I am," Nell countered. "And if I am remembering only the good things, I guess I'm grateful for that."

"Fair enough. Go on."

"I'd make eggs Benedict for me and Joel and pancakes in the shape of angels for the girls. Later in the day our neighbors would bring over a traditional homemade Christmas pudding. They'd lived in the States for years but were originally from England."

"What about church?" Jill asked. "I took Stuart to an Episcopal church for a few years, but he never seemed to enjoy anything about the services, not even at Christmas time. I even enrolled him in Sunday school, but he got kicked out."

"Why?" Nell asked with a laugh. "I'd think you'd have to be pretty naughty to get kicked out of Sunday school. You know, God forgives sinners and all."

"Well, Reverend Moore didn't forgive Stuart for throwing spitballs at him whenever his back was turned. So, what about church?"

"When the girls were little," Nell told her, "I insisted the four of us go to church on Sundays and on Christmas and Easter morning. My parents had been churchgoers, though not in the least bit spiritual, and I'd always enjoyed attending services with them. I loved the concurrent sense of solemnity and joy, and I guess I hoped that my children would inherit my appreciation of ceremony."

"It sounds as if there's a 'but' coming," Jill noted.

"There is," Nell admitted. "One year Joel announced he'd had enough of church. He said that all he did was sit in the pew and think about football, so there was no point in his going. I felt that without Joel something essential had gone out of the tradition, so I stopped attending church as well, eventually even on Christmas. The girls didn't seem to mind."

"Do you miss the church experience?" Jill asked.

Nell thought about the question. She had abandoned church for Joel's sake. He hadn't asked her to, and now Nell wondered if her abandoning so much she had cared for—poetry, religious tradition—had been a manifestation of an innate laziness, as she had hinted to Eric the day before, or evidence of a long-standing inability to respect her own needs and desires. Either was a troubling idea. "Yes," she said finally. "I guess I do." And then Nell had an idea. "Look," she said. "Spend Christmas Day with me and the girls. We'll have a lovely time."

Jill shook her head. "Thanks, Nell, but I know how much you need this holiday season to be very special for the King women. I can't intrude."

"You wouldn't be intruding. Come on. I'm not letting you sit alone in your house while we're down the road feasting. Please."

"I won't be alone," Jill countered. "I can invite myself to my cousin's house in Bangor."

Nell put her hands on her hips. "Jill. You don't even like him and you can't stand his wife. Didn't she serve moldy meat the last time you were there?"

"All right," Jill said with a grateful smile. "Thank you. It means a lot to me to share Christmas with your family. Hey, are those cookies cool enough to eat? I'm not sure how much longer I can hold out."

"Help yourself. I'll make a pot of tea."

"While you're doing that, you can tell me how things are going with Eric. Oh my God these cookies are fantastic."

"They're not *going* anywhere," Nell corrected quickly. "But I am really enjoying spending time with him again. I—"

"You what? Come on, spill."

Nell put the kettle on the stove before answering. "Yesterday Eric told me that he believes in me. It was regarding my writing, but somehow I got the feeling he was also speaking in more general terms. What I can't understand is what he sees in me that inspires belief."

"He sees what he saw all those years ago," Jill said firmly. "Look, Nell, it seems to me you're doing it again, devaluing yourself just like you did when your parents told you that Eric was no good and that your feelings for him were wrong and misplaced. You *knew* the truth but didn't trust what you knew."

"Maybe, but I've done so little with my life, Jill, besides raising my children."

"Eric sees *you*, not a résumé of accomplishments. Why is that so hard to accept? Love has nothing to do with performance or status. People fall in love all the time *just because*."

"I didn't say he was in love with me," Nell protested. "Just that he believes in me."

"Is that really so different? Hey, where's that tea?"

"Ready to pour," Nell said. "And there's one more thing I want to tell you. Molly broke things off with Mick this morning and not in a very nice way. I think she just snapped."

Jill shook her head. "This holiday season is just full of surprises, isn't it? How is she?"

"Miserable, I assume, though she won't talk to me yet."

"Poor kid, and she really is just a kid."

"I was thinking the same thing the other day," Nell told her. "I was thinking of how at her age I made a decision spectacularly against my own interest. Youth is a dangerous time."

"It is indeed." Jill finished her tea and reached for her sweater, hung over the back of a chair. "Well, you know where to find me if you want to talk more. Just bring some of those raspberry cookies when you visit."

When Jill had let herself out, Nell thought about what her friend had said. Was believing in someone the same as loving them? It wasn't inconceivable that Eric could love her for the sake of the past; in fact, it was probable. But that wasn't the same as loving her in the present.

Or could it be?

Chapter 23

"Why did you make eggnog from scratch?" Felicity asked, peering into her glass. The glass was one of a set of nine Nell had found in a local thrift shop. Felicity's was decorated with an image of Rudolph the red-nosed reindeer. Nell's glass featured Comet.

"Homemade is usually better than store bought," Nell said.

"Yeah, but it's definitely a lot easier to buy something than to make it from scratch."

Nell sliced through the tape sealing a cardboard box of ornaments. "Easier isn't always better."

Felicity took another sip from her glass. "Well, it is pretty delicious. Hey, what's with Molly? She's been in her room all day. I don't even know what Mick brought by this morning."

"He brought a very pretty print of seven swans," Nell told her. "I put it against the wall behind the tree for safe-keeping."

Felicity put her glass on the coffee table. "Maybe I should get Molly to join us."

"I'll go," Nell said hurriedly. A moment later she knocked

on her daughter's door. "Molly?" she called. "We're about to trim the tree."

Molly opened the door a sliver but wouldn't meet her mother's eyes. Her own eyes were red and swollen from crying. "I can't, Mom," she said very quietly. "Sorry."

"It might make you feel better not to be alone right now," Nell said gently.

"I'm fine. Look, don't tell Fliss what happened this morning. Not yet."

"All right. Will you be down for dinner? I'm making that eggplant dish you love, the one with the melted mozzarella on top."

Molly shook her head. "I don't know. I'm not hungry."

"Okay," Nell said. "Just let me know if you want to talk."

Molly nodded and closed the door to her room. Nell stood where she was for a moment, swamped again by that awful feeling of futility, helpless to do or to say anything that might bring a smile of genuine happiness to her child's face. Slowly, she returned to the living room. "Your sister doesn't feel well," she told Felicity. "She said we should start without her."

Nell began to decorate the giant tree, carefully hanging ornaments the family had collected through the years. *Christmas without X means Christmas with Y*, she thought. *Next Christmas, decorating the tree without the help of the girls will mean* . . . But again Nell's imagination failed her. Decorating the tree had always been a family occasion. Even Joel had joined in the fun, first stringing the tree with lights and then lifting the girls on his shoulders so they could hang ornaments on the higher branches.

"Earth to Mom?"

Nell startled. "What? Sorry, Fliss. My mind wandered."

"I asked if you want me to put the star on top. I know you don't like heights."

"If you would, Fliss," Nell said with a grateful smile. "Thank you."

"No problem. I'll get the stepladder."

While Felicity went to fetch the stepladder from the kitchen pantry, Nell looked at the ornament she had just taken from its tissue paper wrapping. It was a Swarovski crystal snowflake, a gift from Joel on the last Christmas they had spent as husband and wife. There was a strong possibility that Joel had already begun his affair with Pam before that holiday season. Still, Nell hung the crystal snowflake with care. The past could be honored even when in retrospect it appeared slightly tarnished. Nell truly believed that.

"I'm glad you were free this evening," Eric said. "My work habits are so quirky I sometimes forget that not everyone has the luxury of sleeping in of a morning if they happen to have been out the night before."

Nell smiled. "And not everyone has the pressure of writing hugely popular novels to a contracted deadline."

"Work is work," Eric said. "It's all important."

"And eight o'clock isn't so very late to meet," Nell noted. Still, she had been a bit nervous that Felicity might pelt her with questions when she announced that she was meeting a colleague from Mutts and Meows for a holiday drink. But Felicity had simply shrugged and gone to her room. Molly remained behind her closed door, her dinner waiting to be reheated in the microwave if she found an appetite.

Nell and Eric were seated at the marble-topped bar at the Good Angel. A tall white Christmas tree had pride of place in a corner of the room. It was hung with sparkly silver and blue ornaments. Swaths of what looked like white silk were draped along the mantel over the stately marble fireplace. Even the tablecloths and tableware were on theme; the cloths were red and the plates decorated with a border of mistletoe.

"The new owners have really gone all out," Nell commented.

"Clearly they have high hopes for Christmas being a season of financial success. Too bad holidays come with so many unreasonable expectations. We're all bound to be disappointed when the reality doesn't match the dream."

"True," Nell agreed. "Do you want to know the one thing that's most disappointed me about the Christmas season? The fact that I was never able to get a picture of the girls on Santa Claus's lap."

"What do you mean you weren't able?" Eric asked, taking a sip of his Irish coffee.

"I mean that I tried and failed," Nell explained. "I had a picture taken of Molly with Santa before Felicity was born, but somehow it got lost. So when Felicity was old enough, I took both girls to the Copley Plaza mall with the intention of having their picture taken with Santa. I dressed them in red velvet skirts with white blouses and white stockings and black patent leather Mary Janes."

"Sounds sufficiently adorable," Eric noted.

"It was, before Felicity threw up on Santa before the photographer could shoot. Santa was not amused."

Eric laughed. "Not as jolly as you could have wished?"

"Not by half. The next year I tried again. Everything was going smoothly until Molly spotted some awful little plastic doll in the window of a store and demanded we stop and buy it. I said no and Molly pouted and by the time I had wrangled the girls into the line of people waiting their turn with Santa she was in the midst of a full-blown tantrum. The supervising elves asked us to leave. The strange thing was it was the first and only time Molly ever threw a tantrum."

"Did you try the next year?" Eric asked.

"I would have," Nell told him, "but both girls were down with a bad flu for the two weeks before Christmas, so I lost my opportunity. Then the following year Molly announced that she didn't believe in Santa Claus and that there was no way she was going to sit on a 'fake guy's' lap. I thought she was a little young to be so disillusioned, but she was very serious about it. I considered taking Felicity alone, but for so long I'd had my heart set on a photo of the two girls with Santa that I decided to throw in the proverbial towel." Nell smiled. "The girls laugh at me. They think I'm being too sentimental when I remind them that I'm probably the only mother in the USA who cares about such things who doesn't have a picture of her children with Santa Claus."

"My mother's got a picture of Sarah and me with Santa," Eric told her. "And every year she puts it on the mantel. And every year my sister brings her sons to the mall for their photo op."

"See? It's become an important holiday tradition!" Nell took a sip of her red wine before going on. "Do you remember the Christmas you came to my house?"

Eric nodded. "Of course."

"My parents behaved so badly. I'll never forget how my mother managed to avoid looking you in the eye the entire time and how my father grilled you about your grades and your plans for the future. And you were so good about it all, so even tempered. When you'd gone home, I tried to tell them how disappointed and embarrassed I was, but . . . Well, I never could stand up to my parents. I got as far as saying something like 'you could have been nicer,' to which my mother said something like, 'whatever do you mean?' and that was the end of my protest."

Eric took her hand for a moment. "It's okay," he said. "You were more far more negatively affected than I was. I seem to be able to block a good deal of the nastiness people throw at each other. A gift or a curse, the fact is that I'm remarkably resilient and stubbornly optimistic."

Resiliency and optimism. Two very good qualities to have when one is facing an uncertain future, Nell thought. *Like an empty home.*

"Molly broke up with her boyfriend of almost six years this morning." Nell hadn't intended on telling this to Eric; the words had just come out. "She's in a muddle about her life, and the crisis has come to a head now, just days before Christmas. Talk about smashed expectations."

"I'm sorry," Eric said. "She must feel awful."

"She does. And this might be Felicity's last Christmas at home, at least for a while. She's been invited to join her father and stepmother in Switzerland next year. It's all she can talk about."

"And you're not happy about it," Eric observed.

"Not really," Nell admitted, "but I know I'm being selfish. If spending Christmas with her father will make Felicity happy, then she should take the opportunity." Nell shook her head. "I'm sorry. I don't know why I'm telling you all this. You don't want to hear about my domestic woes."

"I want to hear about your *family.* Just because I don't have kids of my own doesn't mean I'm not interested in other people's children."

"I didn't mean to imply that you weren't," Nell said hastily. "I've read your books. I've seen how you can so perfectly imagine all sorts of lives."

Eric laughed. "I don't know about perfectly, but I do try. And anyway, we're friends, aren't we?"

Nell nodded. "Yes. I suppose we are friends."

"And friends share their thoughts and feelings, their desires and disappointments. Right?"

Desires and disappointments. "Right." Nell looked at her watch. "I should be getting home. It's my turn to open the clinic tomorrow."

Eric paid for their drinks and linked his arm through hers as they left the restaurant. When they got outside they found a dark sky bright with stars.

"There are few sights in this world that give me such a profound sense of peace as a clear night sky." He smiled. "Not a very original sentiment, but true all the same."

Nell felt a remarkable sense of contentment at that moment, standing arm in arm with the man who was perhaps the dearest friend she had ever known.

"Hey," she said suddenly. "Why no puffer coat tonight? You must be freezing in just that sweater and leather jacket."

"I spilled coffee all over it earlier. I washed it as best I could in the bathtub, but it's still drying out."

"The hotel could probably have tossed it in one of their washing machines," Nell pointed out. "It could have been warm and dry by now."

Eric sighed dramatically. "Sadly, that thought didn't occur to me."

Nell laughed. "Next time you have a laundry crisis, call me."

"It's a deal," Eric said, and he drew her into his arms.

Nell rested her head on his shoulder for a moment until she felt him shiver. "You need to get home," she said, reluctantly pulling away.

"Talk tomorrow?" he asked.

Nell smiled and nodded. She watched as Eric walked to his car. Then she got into her own car and turned on the radio. Frank Sinatra was singing "The Christmas Waltz," and Nell found herself singing along as she drove toward her home on Trinity Lane. *'It's that time of year when the world falls in love . . .'*

Chapter 24

Nell was in that state of semi-awareness that comes shortly before sleep, so when she heard the door to her room slowly creak open she thought that she might be imagining the sound. But when she heard Molly whisper: "Mom? Can I come in?" she hoisted herself to a sitting position and reached for the lamp on her bedside table. "Of course," she said, glancing at the clock by the lamp. It was well after midnight.

Nell was alarmed by her daughter's appearance. Molly looked as if she had aged from a fresh-faced girl to a time and experience–ravaged middle-aged woman in the space of less than twenty-four hours. Her complexion was ashen; there were faint but visible lines at the corners of her mouth, and her usually bright blue eyes seemed dulled.

Molly sat on the edge of the bed, and Nell reached for her hand. And although Nell felt sorry that her daughter was struggling, she was also pleased that Molly had come to her in her moment of need. There it was again, that difficult tension between letting a child go and keeping her close.

"I can hardly believe what happened this morning,"

Molly began. "The look on Mick's face when . . . when I told him I didn't love him. It was . . . Why did I lie? Oh, Mom!"

Nell opened her arms, and Molly fell against her, sobs racking her shoulders. Nell smoothed her daughter's hair and waited until the tempest had calmed before speaking.

"Why don't you reach out to Mick?" she suggested.

Molly extricated herself and wiped her cheeks with her palms. "Right now? It's the middle of the night."

"Why not right now?" Nell argued. "This is no time to stand on ceremony."

Molly was silent for a long moment. Finally she said: "I'll send him a text. I'll tell him that I'm sorry and that I didn't mean what I said. I'll tell him that I love him."

"And when the two of you talk, you need to be honest with him regarding your fears about the future."

"I know," Molly admitted. "So, you really think Mick will want to talk to me?"

"I do," Nell said. "And you should tell your sister what happened. She cares about you. She'll want to help."

"I doubt Fliss can do anything, but I'll tell her in the morning," Molly promised. Suddenly, she looked around the room as if seeing it for the first time. "Mom? Why aren't there any Christmas decorations in here?"

Nell remembered what Jill had said about her habit of undervaluing herself, but she could see no benefit in sharing that observation with Molly at this moment. "I guess I just ran out of steam by the time I'd decorated the rest of the house," she said lightly.

"Oh. Gosh, I'm so tired. Good night, Mom."

Nell gave her daughter's hand a final squeeze and watched as Molly left the room. When she was gone, Nell turned out the light and lay back against the pillows, suddenly bothered by a pang of conscience. Maybe she shouldn't have encouraged Molly to believe that Mick would want to reconcile; sometimes damage done could not be undone. But the thought of the young man Nell had been so glad to welcome to her family suddenly being gone from their lives seemed too awful a thing to consider.

Please, she prayed. *Let things be okay for Molly, whatever okay means. Please.*

Chapter 25

Nell placed a plate of bacon on the table. As far as she knew Molly had not eaten anything since the previous morning, and it was a rare person, other than a vegan or vegetarian, who could resist the temptation of bacon. But Molly didn't even glance at the plate.

Felicity frowned at her sister. "Do you feel any better this morning?" she asked. "You look kind of pale."

Molly sighed, looked to her mother and then back to her sister. "I broke up with Mick yesterday."

"You what?" Felicity cried, setting her glass of orange juice on the table with enough force to cause the liquid to splash over the rim. "Why?"

Nell wiped up the spill with her napkin and waited for Molly to respond. When she didn't, Felicity went on.

"I know you said you were going to move to Boston for a while, but you never said anything about breaking up with Mick!"

"I didn't say anything to you, but I was thinking it. And I told Mom. It's just that I've been confused lately . . ."

"What do you mean *confused*?" Felicity pressed.

"Fliss, maybe we shouldn't—"

"It's okay, Mom." Molly sighed. "The thing is, I don't really want to move away. And I *do* love Mick, and I told him so in a text last night and one this morning. But he hasn't gotten back to me, so how can I convince him?"

"In person," Felicity said firmly. "You'll just have to see him face to face. This is not a time to rely on social media. Too many misunderstandings, and it's never entirely private."

"But what if he refuses to see me?" Molly covered her eyes with her hands. "Oh, what have I done?"

"It's only been twenty-four hours, Molly," Nell said gently. "Give him time."

"What did you do with the ring?" Felicity asked.

Molly put her hands in her lap and replied dully. "It's in my dresser. I know I have to return it, but I'm not sure how."

"Why do you have to return it?" Felicity asked. "If you tell Mick you're sorry and he believes you, he'll want you to keep the ring."

"Will he?" Molly shook her head. "Anyway, I feel guilty about having it with the way things stand."

"I suppose you could mail it to him," Felicity suggested. "Though that seems kind of cold. And sending it back might only reinforce the message you gave him—that you don't love him—when you really *do* love him." Felicity frowned. "It's very confusing. What do you think, Mom?"

"I think that Molly should do nothing for the moment," Nell said. "I think she should just breathe deeply and wait."

The rest of breakfast passed in an unhappy silence. Finally the girls went off to school, and Nell prepared to leave for work. She took up her car keys and bag and headed for the front door. As she passed through the living room, she noticed that a window shutter had broken off the gingerbread house. The velvet ribbon tied around one of the pillar candles on the mantel had loosened and slipped. Three of the tiny lights on the string wound around the standing lamp by the chintz-covered easy chair had gone out.

Tears sprang to Nell's eyes. Were all of her efforts at making this Christmas absolutely perfect for her daughters destined to fail? Was every attempt to create an atmosphere of joy to end in a cruel deception? She knew she was overreacting, but at that moment these minor calamities seemed signs of some larger catastrophe awaiting her family this holiday season. Happiness could be so terribly elusive, and even if one was fortunate enough to possess happiness it could be so terribly fleeting.

Which is why one should appreciate whatever bit of happiness presents itself, she thought as she opened the front door and stepped out into the December morning. It was advice worth remembering.

The hours spent at Mutts and Meows had served to distract Nell from the troubles waiting at home. One of her favorite clients had come by for his annual check-up, a noble German shepherd named Roger, and the staff had been introduced to four three-week-old kittens born to a calico named Annabelle who had once famously survived an attack by a fisher cat and a life-saving surgery that resulted.

Now home, Nell was further intent upon keeping sadness at bay by focusing on another Christmas craft. On the kitchen table a magazine was open to a page of instructions for making pomander balls. Nell had laid out the components: several large fresh oranges and lemons; a coil of narrow red-velvet ribbon; small bowls filled with ground cinnamon, ginger, nutmeg, and cardamon; a jar of whole cloves; and a plastic container of orrisroot powder. For holiday ambience Nell had tuned the old-fashioned radio that lived next to the toaster to a station that was playing nothing but classic holiday songs and carols.

"It smells so good in here," Felicity said. "All these Christmasy spices. I wonder what sort of holiday desserts we'll have in Switzerland next year. I should read up on traditional foods. There's got to be a lot more than fondue."

"Let's hope so," Nell said. Before she could suggest that Felicity research a few vegetable options, the front door opened, and a moment later Molly joined them in the kitchen. Her big blue scarf was still wound around her neck and her cheeks were flushed with cold.

"The temperature dropped again," she said. "I'll bring in more wood for the fireplace later."

"Thank you. How were classes?" Nell asked.

"Fine," Molly said, leaning against the counter by the radio. "Not that I could concentrate all that well. Mick still hasn't been in touch."

"I'm sorry. Give him time."

"He'll come around," Felicity added.

Molly ignored the words of support. "What are you guys doing?" she asked.

"We're making pomander balls," Felicity told her sister. "You hang them in a closet."

"So your clothes can smell like nutmeg?" Molly asked. "I definitely smell nutmeg."

"And cinnamon," Nell added. "And citrus. You can also put them in your linen closet to freshen the sheets and towels. The scent can last for years if you sprinkle the balls with orrisroot powder. It acts as a preservative."

Molly managed a smile. "Orrisroot powder? It sounds

like something the witches in *Macbeth* might use in one of their midnight concoctions."

"Pomander is from the French term *pomme d'ambre*," Felicity said. "That means apple of amber. Doesn't that sound pretty? Originally, people carried pomanders as protection against infection in times of plague. It didn't work, of course, but people believed it did. Pomanders were also used to mask bad smells. Basically it was an early form of aromatherapy. Ow! These cloves are sharp!"

Nell glanced at the magazine by her left elbow. "The instructions suggest you use a pin or a nail to make the holes before inserting the cloves."

"I wish I had known that before we started! I'll go find a pin." Felicity dashed over to the junk drawer beneath the microwave and returned a moment later with a paper clip. "This should do," she said.

Molly came over to the table, picked up the little bowl of cinnamon, and sniffed. "Mick's mom would probably like these," she said.

"You could make one for her," Nell suggested.

"Why?" Molly laughed grimly. "I'm sure Mrs. Williams wants nothing to do with me."

"You could give it to her as a sort of peace offering," Felicity suggested.

"But how would that change anything between me and Mick? She's not going to accept a gift from the girl who broke her son's heart. Anyway, Mick probably hates me."

"I'm sure Mick doesn't hate you," Nell said gently.

"Mick wouldn't hate anyone," Felicity added.

"Well, he can't much like me right now."

Before Nell could protest this, Felicity said, "Sssh! It's the weather report."

The three women turned toward the radio as if looking at it would allow them to hear more clearly. And what they heard was that temperatures were dropping severely, as Molly had noted, and a massive snowstorm was predicted in the near future. The usual warnings and caveats were given.

"At least it hasn't become a blizzard warning," Nell said when the newscaster had finished delivering his report and Nat King Cole was singing a holiday song. "Yet. Anyway, we're stocked up on groceries and batteries and water. And I checked that the backup generator is working. If we're stranded, at least we'll be stranded in comfort."

"I think the idea of a big snowstorm on Christmas is kind of romantic," Felicity said. "We can sit around a roaring fire and light candles and tell ghost stories. Like in the lyrics of that song they played before, 'we'll tell tales of the glories of Christmases long, long ago.' "

"Storms are not fun or romantic," Molly said fiercely. "Do you know how many accidents happen due to people mishandling backup gas generators? Do you know how many people die of heart attacks from shoveling snow? Think about Mick's situation. The farm buildings are all winterized, but animals are just as prone to hypothermia and frostbite as we are. And Mick's father has heart trouble. What if Gus tries to do too much and . . ." Molly took off her glasses and wiped tears from her eyes.

Felicity looked stricken. "I'm sorry, Molly. I didn't mean to ignore the realities."

"No I'm sorry," Molly said. "I didn't mean to snap. I'm going to my room."

When Molly had left the kitchen, Felicity looked to her mother. "This is awful, Mom. What are we going to do? It's like the *worst* time of the year for someone to break up. Everyone's singing about being happy and in love and giving gifts, and half of the commercials on TV are for jewelry stores and engagement rings. If I were Molly I'd want to lock myself in my room and not come out until the middle of January."

Nell sighed. "I really don't know what we're going to do, Fliss. I wish I did, but I don't."

Chapter 26

About forty minutes later Nell opened the front door to find Jill, holding out a wreath made of dried flowers and herbs. "Here," she said. "This is for you. Not like you need another wreath, but I found myself with some spare hours on my hands. Until Brian died I didn't realize just how much time we spent together. He's left such a gaping hole in my life . . ." Jill smiled ruefully. "And I'm filling it with dried flowers."

Like I'm filling the anticipated hole in my life with butter and sugar and glitter and ribbon, Nell thought.

"Come in," Nell said. Together the women walked to the kitchen. "Felicity and I made pomander balls earlier. Here, this one is for you."

Jill accepted the gift and inhaled deeply. "Mmm. Thank you, Nell. I think I'll keep this on my bedside table. Maybe the scents will bring me pleasant dreams."

"If that works, let me know. Poor Molly is miserable. I don't know if I should call Mary Williams and try to explain the situation."

"How can you explain something you don't understand?" Jill asked.

"There is that. But maybe I should reach out to her, offer, I don't know, sympathy."

Jill shook her head. "I'm not sure that's a good idea. Nothing's really settled between Molly and Mick, is it? They've been together too long to let the relationship go without a struggle. Okay, Mick's gone silent, but I doubt that will last, and you don't want to muddy the waters by interfering."

"Maybe you're right," Nell admitted. "But what if Mary reaches out to me? We've been such good neighbors to each other since just after the girls and I moved to Yorktide."

"Not to resort to a cliché, but old-time Mainers are a fairly reticent breed. Stoic, too. I don't expect Mary will be phoning any time soon to discuss her son's personal business. And I doubt she'd much welcome anyone, well, like I said, anyone interfering."

Nell sighed. "What a mess."

"And not your mess to clean up," Jill pointed out. "It's tough to let a child go, but it's something you *have* to do, for her sake as well as for yours."

"I know," Nell admitted. "And frankly, I've been wondering how pure my motives are. Do I want Molly to marry Mick because I believe that's what will really make her happy? Or do I want her to marry Mick because it will make *me* happy?"

"Good question. On another note, how is your Mr. Manville?" Jill asked.

"He's hardly *mine*."

"Just an expression."

"I know. He's fine. When we met last night we agreed that we're friends. I'm happy about that."

Jill looked at Nell closely. "Are you falling in love?" she asked.

"How can I be?" Nell replied promptly. "I've got more important things to focus on."

"Of course. When are you seeing him next?"

"I'm meeting him for dinner later."

"Have you told the girls about him yet?"

"No."

"Why?" Jill asked.

Nell laughed a bit and shrugged. "It doesn't seem relevant."

"By which you mean it seems irrelevant. That's an interesting choice of words to use in relation to telling your children about someone you consider a friend."

Nell opened her mouth to respond to Jill's observation, but her mind was suddenly blank. What *had* she meant by choosing the words she had chosen? Before she could begin to puzzle out an answer, Jill was heading toward the kitchen door.

"I've got a chicken pot pie in the oven," she said. "Enjoy the evening. And thanks for the pomander ball. My mother used to make these, you know. This will bring back happy memories of when I was her little girl."

When Jill had gone, Nell wrote a note telling Molly and Felicity what she had prepared for their dinner. Once again she fibbed about with whom she would be having her own evening meal. Why *hadn't* she told her daughters about Eric or offered to introduce them now that he was back in her life, if only for a brief time? Could it be that she was unwilling to share a relationship that felt so entirely *hers* and hers alone? That seemed childish if not exactly selfish. But maybe it was true all the same. Whatever the reason, Nell realized, she had better tell Molly and Fliss soon, before someone in town asked them how their mother knew a favorite writer, and they were left struggling for a reply.

* * *

The atmosphere at the Friendly Lobsterman could not be more different than the atmosphere at the Good Angel. Added to the usual photos of local lobstermen dating back to the mid-nineteenth century, the strings of little red lights in the shape of lobsters and clams, and the old wooden lobster traps suspended from the ceiling, plain pine wreaths hung on all four walls of the main dining area and a freshly cut pine tree decorated with red-and-green plaid bows stood in one corner of the room. A Santa hat was perched on the head of the life-size statue of a lobsterman behind the hostess station. Kitschy but fun, Nell thought, and the food was always good and plentiful.

When the waiter had brought their fish and chips and gone off again, Eric asked: "How did you and Joel meet? Okay, that's another blunt question out of the blue."

Nell smiled. "I don't remember how we met," she admitted. "He was always sort of there in the background, the son of my father's business partner. We'd see each other a few times a year at parties and charity events. By the time we started to date not long after you and I broke up . . . Well, our marriage seemed a foregone conclusion. In a way there was no avoiding it. That sounds awful. Of course I had a choice, even if I thought I didn't."

"Free will. Choice. Pretty confusing concepts for us all."

"Agreed. How did you and Katrina meet?" Nell asked.

"At a party given by a mutual acquaintance," Eric told her. "It wasn't long after the publication of my first novel. I think we were drawn to each other because we were both writers and understood things about each other's lives it can be difficult for people working in more regular fields to understand. But like I told you, time proved that we weren't truly compatible. You know, my parents never really took to Katrina. I think the dangerous and very public nature of her work made them feel as if she existed on a higher plane. They used to treat her with a sort of timid deference." Eric smiled. "Thankfully, they still regard me as first and foremost their son. When I visit I'm still required to bring my dirty dishes to the sink after dinner and make my bed in the morning."

Nell smiled. "You're close to your parents."

"Yes. I had a remarkably happy childhood. Sometimes I find it odd that being a person with such a drama-free past I chose to write about domestic tensions."

"And I came from a family of drama—albeit of the quiet sort—and I sought a family life of peace at all costs. Growing up, I often felt my parents were looking at me and thinking, *that's not quite what we ordered, is it?* It's why I set out from the start to make certain that my children felt loved and appreciated for being exactly who they are."

"How do things stand with your parents now?" Eric asked.

"Relations are cool," Nell said. "When Joel left me, my parents suggested I'd brought the divorce upon myself by not having been a good enough wife. I swore I'd always been one hundred percent supportive of Joel and argued that if he was unhappy he should have come to me and we could have dealt with the problem together. But nothing could change their opinion." Nell smiled ruefully. "For a short time I wondered if my parents were right and that maybe I had in some way been responsible for Joel's bad behavior. Luckily, I came to my senses. For the sake of the girls I maintain contact, but increasingly we see less and less of Grandma and Grandpa Emerson."

"Understandable," Eric said firmly.

"Frankly," Nell went on, "Molly and Felicity were never

particularly close to my parents. In fact, the only grandparent who ever showed them real warmth was Joel's mother, Josephine. Josie was furious with her son for leaving his wife and children. She told me that Joel's father, Lawrence, had had several mistresses over the course of their marriage but that she had turned a blind eye because she knew he would never abandon his family. She felt that Joel shouldn't have allowed the relationship with his mistress to damage his marriage."

Eric whistled. "I'm not sure I know what to say to that. I've sunk a character or two in a marriage of extreme compromise, but when you encounter that sort of domestic dynamic in real life, well, it makes you feel a bit woozy."

"Yes," Nell agreed. "But hearing Josie's story helped me understand more about Joel's poor paternal role model. When Josie died, about a year after the divorce, I felt as if I'd lost my one genuine ally in the family. She was a good woman. She chaperoned Molly and Felicity at Joel's wedding to Pam."

"What's the old goat Lawrence up to these days?" Eric asked.

"Married to a woman twenty-four years his junior. I last saw him at Josie's funeral and Joel doesn't have much more contact with him. Joel and Pam weren't even invited to Lawrence's wedding."

Eric shook his head. "Happy families are all the same . . . Hey, listen. Hear this? It's my favorite goofy Christmas song. 'Grandma Got Run Over by a Reindeer.' "

"Poor Grandma!" Nell laughed. "Thanks for listening to tales of my wacky family."

"My pleasure," he said. "And I promise you won't find any of the more colorful Kings or Emersons in my books."

Eric excused himself to visit the gents', and while he was gone Nell entertained an odd thought. If one day she and

Eric were to marry, she would definitely be getting the better end of the bargain as far as in-laws went. *Poor Eric,* she thought. *What a rotten deal that would be for him. And how awkward it would be for Mom and Dad!* And then she shook her head. It was a preposterous thought, she and Eric marrying. Almost as preposterous as Grandma getting run over by Santa and one of his reindeer.

Chapter 27

Nell was sitting at the table with a bowl of small Styrofoam balls, several plastic tubes of glitter, a packet of screw-in hooks, and a large squeeze bottle of Elmer's glue when Felicity came into the kitchen.

"Glitter balls?" she said, going to the fridge and taking out a carton of low-fat yogurt.

Nell smiled. "How did you guess?"

"How many tubes of glitter did you buy this season anyway?"

"Five. No wait, six. Red, silver, blue, green, gold, and white. Hey, did I hear you on the phone a few minutes ago?"

"Yeah," Felicity said, joining Nell at the table. "I was talking to Dad. I called to tell him I changed my mind about spending Christmas with him in Switzerland next year."

Nell was stunned. She put the cap on the tube of glitter she had been using; her hands were shaking enough to cause a spill. "But you were so looking forward to the trip," she said. "Did something happen? Did your father or Pam say something to put you off the idea?"

Felicity shrugged. "No. It was my decision. I thought you'd be happy, Mom."

"Well, I am happy but . . . You're not backing out of the trip because you think I'll be sad spending Christmas without you? I mean, I would be sad, but that's my concern, not yours."

"No, this is my own decision, and it's all about me." Felicity laughed. "Wait. That sounds horrible. What I mean is that I love Christmas here at home."

"But what about the skiing and the fondue and the sauna and the gorgeous Italian guys?"

Felicity sighed. "Okay, you want the whole story?"

"Yes," Nell said. "I do."

"When Molly started talking about moving to Boston," Felicity began, "I started to think a lot about wanting change just for the sake of change. It made me wonder if maybe Molly wanted to leave Yorktide because she thought it was something she *should* do and not really something she *wanted* to do. I don't know the answer to that question. Only Molly knows—or she will know someday. And then when Molly broke up with Mick, who was like the love of her life, I started to think about how easy it is to lose track of what matters most to you. I started to ask myself why I was so excited about spending Christmas with Dad and Pam and Taylor next year, and what I realized was that Dad and Pam and Taylor weren't the attraction. I think I just wanted to be able to tell my friends I was jetting off to Switzerland to ski with a former Olympic champion who just happens to be my stepmother. I realized that the glamour of the whole thing kind of blinded me, and that's not cool. I mean, it's not a crime or anything, but I thought I was more mature than to turn my back on what really matters to me—my home—just so I could brag about hanging out with a bunch of rich people who don't know me and who probably don't want to know me." Felicity shrugged. "It's like that old saying.

Sometimes what you really want is right in front of you but you're too close to see it. Or something like that."

Nell fought back tears of pride. "I'm impressed," she said feelingly. "It takes courage to examine your motives and find them lacking. Did you explain all this to your father?"

"No," Felicity admitted. "I didn't want to hurt him, so I just told him I'd changed my mind because I really love being at home at Christmas. It's the truth, just not the whole truth."

"You'll miss hanging out with Pam."

"Not really," Felicity said. "Pam's okay but she's not you, Mom. She can be a drama queen. She's used to getting attention after all these years in the spotlight. I kind of wish I hadn't said yes to the Rolex, but Dad said she'll be disappointed I'm not going away with them next year so I'd probably only hurt her feelings if I said no to the watch, too."

"That's kind of you," Nell said. She had met Joel's wife only once. It was during the days of the divorce, and it was clear that Pam was as uncomfortable with the meeting as Nell was. The few minutes Nell had spent in her presence had proved to be a step toward acceptance of the woman Joel had chosen over his family. The caricature Nell had imagined of the evil mistress was replaced by the far more realistic image of a flesh-and-blood human being—indeed a mother—with both strengths and weaknesses. The woman might be a diva but she wasn't evil or unfeeling. "So, want to make a few glitter balls with me?" Nell asked her daughter.

"Sure. Pass me the green and the blue? I want to mix the colors. You know," Felicity blurted a moment later. "I can't stop thinking about Mick. He's like part of the family. How are we supposed to get along without him? But we can't stay friends with him, because that would be a betrayal of Molly. Doesn't she realize what she's doing to us by ending their relationship?"

"She's not thinking about anyone other than herself right now," Nell explained, "and not very clearly at that. Don't be mad at her."

"I'm not mad, Mom, really. Just—worried."

"Me, too," Nell admitted.

Felicity squeezed a ribbon of glue onto a Styrofoam ball and sprinkled the blue-and-green glitter mixture along it. "I keep thinking about all the times the Williams family came through for us," she said, "and about all the times we came through for them. Is that all over now? Are we supposed to stop being nice to each other?"

"I don't know how it will work from here on in," Nell admitted. "The same thought has been on my mind, too. Remember before we had two cars and my old Mazda broke down? Gus gave me the loan of one of his pickup trucks while my car was in the shop. It was awfully nice of him."

"And remember when Mrs. Williams had emergency surgery and had to stay in the hospital for six days? If it weren't for us bringing Mick and his father meals, they would have starved." Felicity laughed. "I thought everyone knew how to use a microwave, but those two were pathetic!"

"Spoiled is more like it. Are you done with the green glitter?"

Felicity passed the tube to her mother. "Relationships are so fragile, aren't they? It's so hard to count on anyone staying together. I mean first you and Dad, and then Molly and Dad, and now Molly and Mick, and maybe you and me and Mr. and Mrs. Williams."

"Yes," Nell said. "But the three of us will always have each other. You, Molly, and me."

"And we'll have Dad," Felicity added. "I mean, I will and Molly *can* if she wants to."

And in a way, Nell thought, *I'll always have Joel, too.* That wasn't a bad thing.

"What do you think?" Felicity asked, holding her glitter ball aloft by the hook. "Kind of psychedelic."

"I like it."

Felicity rose from the table. "Mom? How many more of these things are you going to do?"

Nell surveyed the pile of sparkly ornaments on the table. "Just two or three more."

"The tree is already decorated," Felicity pointed out. "There isn't room for even one more ornament on it."

"I suppose I could buy another small tree and—"

"Mom!" Felicity groaned dramatically. "Three trees are enough! You're obsessed! By the way, I sent Molly a text telling her I'll be around for Christmas next year. I thought she should know right away. I'm not sure why I thought it might help, but . . . See you later, Mom." Felicity gave her mother's cheek a quick peck and left the kitchen.

Obsessed with Christmas. Nell decided right then that after the holidays she would donate a good many of the ornaments she had made or bought in the past weeks to the hospital's pediatric unit. And about that designer handbag Felicity wanted for Christmas. Well, now Nell knew for sure what she should have known all along, that she didn't have to bribe her daughter with expensive goods to win her love. She already had her daughter's devotion and as of this moment she would stop comparing herself to Pam Bertrand-King and finding herself lacking. After all, could Pam make such perfect daughters? Nell thought not.

"So she really told her father she wasn't going to Switzerland with him next December?" Jill asked.

Nell's cell phone was on speaker mode. Her hands were busy forming crescent cookies. "She did."

"Wow. Okay, not to burst your bubble or anything, but Felicity could change her mind again. And one day she will indeed be gone."

Nell rolled her eyes. "I know that. I'm not entirely in denial, Jill."

"I didn't say that you were. So, how was dinner with Eric?"

"The fish and chips were delicious."

"Not the food, silly."

"It was a lovely evening."

"Are you *sure* a romance isn't budding?"

"Yes," Nell said quickly. "I'm sure."

"Look," Jill went on, "I know the idea of a relationship is scary, but you can't allow yourself to feel guilty for finally wanting something just for *you*."

"I don't feel guilty," Nell protested. "It's just that nothing romantic is happening between Eric and me."

Jill sighed. "Okay, be negative, I can't stop you. See you soon."

I'm not being negative, Nell thought when the call was ended. *I'm just being realistic.* Yes, she loved Eric, and yes, they were friends, but he would be leaving for New York before long. They might become email buddies for a while; they might even talk to each other via phone once or twice. But then the inevitable would happen. Time would pass, and they would drift apart. Eric would meet another woman and fall in love, marry, and maybe even start that family he said he had wanted.

At least I'll have the satisfaction of knowing that he doesn't hate me, Nell thought as she placed a crescent cookie on the baking sheet. *At least I'll have the memories of the days we spent together as friends this Christmas sea-*

son. And those memories would have to be enough to sustain her during the lonely years ahead with the girls gone and the house empty. But there would be poetry, if she allowed there to be. And suddenly Nell remembered something C. S. Lewis had said, words that had given her great encouragement so many years ago. "You can make anything by writing."

As she slid the baking sheet into the oven, Nell felt her spirits lift. She knew the process of crafting a fulfilling future, one in which writing played a significant but not the only part, wouldn't be easy. But it could be done. At least, Nell thought with determination, she could try.

Chapter 28

They had decided to meet again at the Butter Churn. Nell was able to get the same table at which she and Eric had sat before. She had been there almost fifteen minutes before Eric came through the door. The sight of him brought a smile to her face.

"Sorry I'm late," Eric said, joining her. "I usually *am* late, aren't I?"

"Not today," Nell told him. "I got to Kennebunk about a half hour ago so I could spend some time in the cemetery, but it was so cold I had to come inside after a few minutes. Puffer coat still out of action?" she asked, noting that Eric seemed to be wearing three sweaters under his leather jacket. The neck of one of the sweaters was torn.

"I got ketchup on it," he explained. "But this time I asked the hotel if they could clean it. Hey, remember that tiny little cemetery we stumbled on when we took a day trip to Lexington and Concord? Some of the stones were so degraded we had to trace what remained of the writing with our fingers to figure out names and dates."

"I remember. I don't know why people consider cemeteries morbid places, though a lot of the modern ones do look so sadly cold."

"You're a romantic, Nell, as am I. It's one of the reasons we've always got on so well."

Yes, Nell thought. *I am a romantic.* "How was your morning?" she asked when a waiter had taken their order for coffee and a cherry-filled pastry Eric insisted they share.

"Interesting," he said. "I wrote for about an hour and then I hit a snag, so I went to the beach for a long walk. It was so unbelievably beautiful, and it was just the sand, the ocean, the occasional seagull, and me. And some snow. By the time I got back to the hotel I'd gotten myself out of the hole I'd inadvertently dug. That sort of thing never happens when I'm wandering the streets of Manhattan."

"The healing power of nature?" Nell suggested.

Eric nodded. "I wouldn't be surprised."

The waiter appeared with their order, and as Eric sliced the pastry in half he asked Nell how her morning had passed.

"Interesting as well," Nell told him. "Felicity took me completely by surprise when she told me she'd canceled the trip to Switzerland with her father next Christmas. She said she realized just how much she enjoys being home for the holidays."

"Why do you look doubtful?" Eric asked.

"Do I? It's just that I'd like to believe her, but I'm afraid she's giving up what might be an exciting opportunity to spare my feelings."

"Teenagers get a bad rap, don't they?" Eric said. "Not all are totally self-focused. Plenty of them are familiar with making a willing sacrifice. Still, do you think Felicity would lie to you about her motives?"

"Not really," Nell admitted, "but lately there are times

when I feel my daughters are strangers to me. I realize I don't know what they're thinking, and I'm surprised by their decisions."

"Every day they're becoming more autonomous beings."

"I know, and that's the point of raising children, and I would never dissuade either of them from following their dreams." Nell smiled. "But I'm not above trying to get their attention and their gratitude with sugar and crafts. I'm even knitting them Christmas stockings—and I'm a lousy knitter."

"What you're experiencing is totally natural," Eric said. "Which doesn't make it any easier, but at least you know you're not losing your mind."

"But I am losing the role that's been my identity for the past twenty-one years."

"Surely that role won't be gone entirely," Eric argued. "Surely a parent is never done being a parent. Sorry. I don't mean to imply that what you're feeling isn't important. And what do I know about the emotional trauma parents experience when a child leaves home, other than what I've learned while researching."

"You don't need to research to understand universal feelings like love and loss. But I suppose that reading about other people's experiences does give you food for thought."

"Exactly. So, would it be all right if I met Molly and Felicity?" Eric asked. And then he smiled. "Or is this really bad timing on my part?"

"I haven't told them about you," Nell blurted.

"Why not? Do I embarrass you? I have learned how to comb my hair." Eric ran his hand through the loose wild curls. "Sort of."

"Of course not," Nell said hurriedly. "It's just . . ." It

was just, Nell thought, that this renewed friendship with Eric was *not* irrelevant, no matter how casually she had implied just that when talking to Jill. It was anything *but* irrelevant; it was by far the most important thing that had happened to her aside from the birth of her children. And bringing together the most important people of her life . . . Well, the thought was challenging. So much could go so terribly wrong. So much could go so very right. "Why do you want to meet them?" she asked finally.

Eric reached across the table for her hand. "Simple. I knew the old Nell, and now I'm getting to know this Nell. And this Nell has spent the last twenty-one years being a mother, and that makes her in some ways an entirely new person to me."

Getting to know this Nell . . . "I promise to talk to the girls," Nell said promptly. "I'll tell them we're old friends and that you'd like to meet them. They're fans of your work, you know."

Eric grinned. "As long as they don't ask me where I get my ideas. I never know how to answer that question."

"Okay. I'll tell them not to ask. And by the way, where *do* you get your ideas?"

"From the back of cereal boxes," Eric said. "That's my answer and I'm sticking to it. Now, eat your pastry."

Chapter 29

"Thanks for doing the shoveling, Fliss."

Felicity removed another layer of clothing and sank into a chair at the kitchen table. "No worries, Mom. It's good exercise. Besides, we've only gotten a few inches so far."

"There's a lot more predicted," Molly pointed out. "Remember that time a few years back when we were snowed in for three days?"

"Yeah," Felicity said. "Mr. Roberts from the hardware store got lost in that storm. By the time they found him he had frostbite. I heard he lost all ten of his toes."

"Only two toes, Fliss," Molly corrected. "His wife got carried away the more she told the tale. Still, two toes is two toes too many. The cold is dangerous."

Nell turned off the gas under the front left burner and carefully poured boiling water over the teabag in her favorite cup. Now might be a good time to tell the girls about her friendship with Eric. But still she hesitated. To share with her children the fact of her long-ago romance as well as the fact of Eric's being back in her life even temporarily was bound to have a big effect, good or bad. She would wait just a little longer.

"We might want to get to the concert early tonight," she said. "I read in the paper there's an important organist scheduled to play a prelude to the program. It might be difficult to get good seats."

Molly, who was at the table sewing a button on a blouse, shook her head. "Sorry, Mom. I can't. I totally forgot that Andrea's party is tonight."

"Will Mick be there?" Felicity asked.

"No. Andrea didn't invite him, given what happened between us." Molly sighed. "I'm so not in the mood for a party, but I promised Andrea I'd be there, and she really helped me out when I was having trouble with a course last spring, so I'm kind of obliged."

"Felicity?" Nell asked. "You're still coming with me, right?"

Felicity scrunched up her face. "Sorry, Mom. I just found out this afternoon there's a one-time screening of *The Ghost and Mrs. Muir* at the old meetinghouse in South Berwick. Ever since I saw it on television when I was eleven I've wanted to see it on a big screen. It's *so* romantic."

"All right then," Nell said with a smile that hid her disappointment. "You two have a good time and drive carefully."

"We always do, Mom," Molly assured her. "I'd better change. I promised Andrea I'd help her set up for tonight."

"And I need to take a shower. I sweat right through my fleece doing the shoveling. Ugh."

Once she was alone Nell realized with a bit of a shock that she couldn't recall the last time she had attended an event on her own, not even a movie at the little Leavitt Theatre in Ogunquit, or a lecture at the Portland Museum of Art, or a workshop at the Strawberry Lane Community Arts Education Center. For a moment she considered asking Jill to go to the concert with her (Eric was booked to host an online forum arranged by his publisher), but then she thought about those websites she had scoured and she decided not to. Instead, she would follow the advice of the experts and embrace independence. She would go to the concert on her own, and she would enjoy the beautiful music and the presence of her friendly neighbors. The community of Yorktide would make a fine companion.

Nell stood across from the Methodist church on an otherwise empty stretch of road. She had dressed with care, going so far as to wear her best dress, a black wool A-line that came to just below her knees, black knee-high boots (with corrugated rubber soles, of course), and the good camel coat she had bought in the early days of her marriage. She had even put on the pair of pearl earrings Joel had given her one anniversary and a white gold necklace that complemented the pearls. Being on one's own was a good thing, she had told herself while dressing. It was normal. It was healthy.

But as Nell watched families and couples and groups of friends stream through the front doors of the church, her spirits began to falter. For the full ten minutes she had been standing there she had seen no one enter the church on his or her own. Was this to be her future, she wondered, to be the odd one out, solitary, looking on as other people lived their lives in the company of loved ones?

I can't do this, she thought. *I know I'm being silly and weak, but I just can't.* Nell turned and hurried down the darkened road to where she had parked her car. Twenty minutes later she was home and in her nightgown and robe, the earrings and necklace once again safely stowed in her jewelry box and the dress zipped into its protective garment bag.

Nell left her bedroom and settled in the book nook to wait for the girls to return home. Only that morning she had determined to take control of her future and look at what had happened by evening. Nell took a deep breath. *Resiliency and optimism,* she thought. *One step at a time. Be gentle with yourself. No journey was ever completed without the occasional detour and misstep.* Nell reached for the book of poems by Wallace Stevens. Reading was what was required.

"How was the concert?" Molly asked.

It was just after eleven o'clock, and Nell and her daughters were gathered in the kitchen. Nell was at the stove, stirring a pot of chocolate. Three large mugs waited to be filled.

"Wonderful," Nell said brightly, pouring the chocolate into the mugs and wondering when she had become such a liar. It was just that she didn't want her daughters to feel sorry for her. Poor Mom. Too timid (if that was the word) to attend a community concert on her own. "How was the party?" she asked, turning to Molly.

"Lame," Molly said. "Half the people Andrea invited didn't show up, so it was just five of us sitting around with all this food pretending to be having a good time when Andrea was really annoyed and Jim and Gary had clearly had a fight before coming over, because they didn't say one word to each other the entire night and Carl kept checking his phone for updates on some hockey game." Molly managed a smile. "And then there was me, missing Mick and feeling miserable. *Not* a fun time."

"Probably more fun than my night," Felicity said. "The projector broke down twice and the meetinghouse was freezing. I was shivering so hard I could hardly hear the dialogue. I probably should have gone to the concert with you after all, Mom."

Nell smiled. "There's always next year."

Molly drained the last of the hot chocolate in her mug. "I'm exhausted," she announced. "I feel I could sleep right through the holidays and into next year."

"It's the sadness and the stress," Felicity said.

Molly smiled ruefully. "I'm aware. Good night, Mom. Fliss."

A moment later, Felicity followed her sister from the kitchen after giving her mother a kiss on the cheek.

Nell put the empty mugs into the dishwasher. *There's always next year.* But would there be? Sure, Felicity had said she wasn't going abroad with her father, but as Jill had pointed out, she might change her mind again. As for Molly, who knew where she would be next December. *I know where I'll be,* Nell thought. *I'll be right here, and Eric, too, will be gone.*

And in that case, Nell thought resolutely, *I had better tell my daughters about him before the opportunity to do so is past.* What really could be so damaging about introducing Eric to Molly and Felicity? He was her kind and good-hearted friend. He was no threat to her family. She would break her long silence in the morning.

Chapter 30

"Mom? Can you give me the key to our safe deposit box? Pam's Rolex came yesterday, and I want to put it somewhere it won't get damaged."

"You're not going to wear it?" Molly asked.

Felicity shrugged. "Nah. It's a bit much for Yorktide. I'll save it for special occasions or something."

"Sure. I'll get the key after breakfast." Nell joined her daughters at the kitchen table and pulled her robe more tightly across her chest. The house was not immune to sneaky drafts of icy air when the temperature dropped below the freezing point, which it had during the early hours of the morning. "So," she said in a feigned casual tone as she poured a cup of coffee. "I've been keeping a secret from you two."

Felicity reached for a piece of toast. "Did we win the lottery?" she asked.

"Nothing so dramatic. You know the writer Eric Manville?"

"Yeah," Felicity said. "He's really good."

Molly nodded. "He has really soulful eyes. Not that that has anything to do with his books. Just saying."

"Well, I knew him back in college," Nell explained. "Recently we've been in touch. In fact, he's staying in Ogunquit at the moment and we've gotten together a few times."

Molly's eyes widened, and she put her coffee cup on the table with a bit of a thud. "You *know* him? I love his books! I was planning to go to the reading at the Bookworm but Maisie Phillips really needed a babysitter at the last minute and I always seem to need the money, so I took the job."

"I can't believe you actually know Eric Manville!" Felicity cried. "*And Then We Drifted* is one of my favorite books ever. So, were you guys good friends or what?"

"Actually," Nell said, "we went out for almost two years. We were going to get married."

Molly shook her head. "Mom, this is huge. Why didn't you ever tell us?"

"It was a long time ago," Nell explained. "And I didn't feel comfortable talking about the serious boyfriend I had before your father and I started to date. I felt it would be a betrayal of the marriage."

"I'm sure Dad had plenty of girlfriends before you, Mom," Molly said. "I've heard him mention at least three. So, wait, does he know you guys were a couple?"

"No. Your father was always aware that Eric and I had been friends, but I didn't see the need to tell him we had been romantically involved."

"So what happened with Eric?" Felicity asked. "Did he break your heart?"

"No." Nell smiled ruefully. "I broke his heart, and my own for that matter, though I wasn't aware of it until later."

"What do you mean?" Molly asked, leaning forward in interest.

"What I mean," Nell said, "is that Grandma and Grandpa weren't at all happy about my relationship with Eric. They put a lot of pressure on me to break it off. They said Eric didn't show promise, by which they meant he hadn't decided on a career path. They said your father was a safer choice of husband. And I finally did what they wanted and broke up with Eric, started dating your father, and then married him. I wasn't very brave back then. I didn't have the courage to follow my heart."

Molly sat back in her chair. "Oh, Mom," she said. "I'm so sorry."

"I'm sorry, too." Felicity snapped her fingers. "Hey, wait a minute. So that's where you've been sneaking off to! You weren't out buying tinsel or powdered sugar those times when I thought you'd be home. You were hanging out with your old boyfriend!"

"I have not been *sneaking off* anywhere," Nell protested a bit guiltily. "I just . . . I just didn't want to advertise to the world that I was spending time with Eric."

"We're not the world, Mom," Molly pointed out. "We're your daughters. And we could easily have found out through the rumor mill. I'm surprised we didn't."

"I'm surprised, too," Nell admitted. "I'm glad I got to tell you myself."

Felicity reached for another piece of toast and the jar of blackberry preserves. "Hey," she said. "Remember when you first told us you used to write poetry and that reading it now was bringing back bittersweet memories. Was it Eric you were thinking of? Was it writing that brought you guys together in the first place?"

"Yes, it was Eric I was thinking of, and no, Eric didn't start to write seriously until years later, but he was always incredibly supportive of my efforts. In a way he was my in-spiration." Nell took a deep breath before going on. "The reason I'm telling you all this now," she said, "is that Eric would like to meet you. He knows you're the most important people in my life."

Neither girl answered immediately. Nell waited nervously as Molly looked to Felicity and then, after a moment, as Felicity nodded to her sister.

"You said he's staying in Ogunquit," Molly said. "Is he by himself? Didn't I read somewhere that he was married to an important journalist?"

"He was married, but not any longer," Nell told them. "And yes, he's on his own."

"Then why don't you invite Eric to spend Christmas Day with us," Felicity suggested.

"I couldn't do that!" Nell blurted.

"Why not?" Molly asked. "No one should be alone on Christmas."

"Are you sure?" Nell asked, looking from one of her daughters to the other and back again. "Really sure?"

Molly reached for her mother's hand. "Mom," she said, "we're not totally dumb. Fliss and I know how important this Christmas is to you, even if we haven't always been acting very sympathetically."

"Hey! What did I do?" Felicity paused. "Oh, wait. I did go on about the Switzerland thing. Sorry."

"We want you to be happy," Molly continued, "and if having Eric Manville here will make you happy, then go for it. Plus I can get an autograph. Do you think he'd mind?"

Nell laughed and squeezed Molly's hand. "Not at all." She felt so very proud of her children at that moment, proud and grateful and happy. She had sorely underestimated her daughters' generosity toward her. Yes, one day both girls would be gone, but Nell would always have memories of moments like this.

"Good. That's settled." Felicity suddenly turned to her sister. "Any word from Mick?" she asked.

Molly shook her head. "No. He can't just continue to ignore me!"

"Yes," Nell said gently. "I'm afraid he can. And until he's ready to face you you're just going to have to accept his position, as difficult as that is to do."

Molly looked down at her plate and frowned. *Molly is an adult,* Nell reminded herself. *She has to learn how to fix her mistakes on her own. She has to learn how to accept the consequences of her actions without my help.*

"So," Nell said. "Last chance to protest. You're sure you're okay with having Eric here for Christmas?"

Molly looked up and managed a smile. "Yes."

Felicity nodded. "Absolutely."

"Thank you," Nell said. "Really, thank you."

Nell looked at her watch. Eric had called earlier to ask if he could stop by the clinic on his way to Portland for a reading at a new independent bookstore. He had a book of poetry in which he thought she might be interested. The poet was a young Ugandan woman being touted as a voice to be heard.

As soon as Nell looked away from her watch, her phone alerted her to a text. Eric was about a minute from the office. Nell grabbed her coat, hat, and mittens and the large box she had brought with her from home. To say that she was nervous about asking Eric to spend Christmas with her family was an understatement. The worst he could say was no, she reminded herself for about the hundredth time that morning.

Nell opened the door to the clinic to see Eric's car slowly approaching along the plowed drive. The drive would have to be plowed again before long. Snow was falling, and the temperature seemed to be stalled in the low twenties. Southern Maine was in for yet another whopper of a storm.

Eric brought the car to a stop. "Lovely weather we're having," he quipped as he climbed out.

"Nice hat," Nell replied. He was wearing one of those intensely goofy hats with earflaps. What made it truly awful was the fact that it was a bilious shade of green. At least the puffer coat had come clean.

"It does the trick. Here," he said, handing her a slim paperback. "I ordered it from Amazon. My copy is back in New York or I would have lent it to you. Maybe we could talk about the work after you've read the poems."

"Thank you," Nell said, slipping the book into the pocket of her coat. "I'd like that. And I have something for you." Nell handed Eric the box.

"What's in this?" he asked with a laugh. "It weighs a ton."

"Treats for your audience. I told you how I've been going a bit crazy with baking this year."

"It's one way to hold an audience captive. Promise them cookies."

"Eric, I told the girls that we're friends," Nell blurted. "I told them you want to meet them, and they invited you to spend Christmas with us."

Eric's eyes widened. "They did? Wow. That's really generous."

"There's no pressure," Nell went on hurriedly. "If you'd rather spend the day on your own or if you have other plans, I perfectly understand. *We* perfectly understand."

"I'm honored. And I'll be there." Eric leaned forward and kissed Nell's cheek. His lips were cold, but Nell didn't care.

"Drive safely," she said.

Eric stowed the box of treats in the backseat of his car and got behind the wheel. Nell watched as he drove away through the rapidly thickening snow. When he was out of sight, she touched her cheek where his lips had been and smiled.

Chapter 31

"Who's coming caroling with me this evening?" Nell asked. "It's the usual group organized by one of the deacons of the Lutheran church." Nell had already decided that if neither of her daughters accompanied her she would go on her own. There would not be a repeat of last night, when she had so cowardly walked away from the concert.

"Not me," Molly said. "Forcing anyone to listen to me sing is cruel and unusual punishment."

"You don't need to have a fantastic voice to go caroling," Nell pointed out. "It's about the spirit of the season."

"But, Mom, it's like ten degrees out! We'll get frostbite!"

"We'll be fine," Nell assured Felicity. "We've got plenty of cold weather gear. Plus walking from house to house will keep us warm."

Felicity sighed. "All right, but only for an hour. Then we come home and defrost. Where do we meet the others?"

"Outside the post office at seven. Molly?"

Molly shook her head. "Sorry, Mom, but you can count me out and not only because of my voice. I know Mrs.

Williams goes caroling every year with that group. I won't be able to face her."

"You'll have to face her some time," Felicity pointed out reasonably.

"But it doesn't have to be now." Molly turned to leave the kitchen. "Have a good time," she said, and then she was gone.

"What happens if Mick's mother *is* there tonight?" Felicity asked quietly.

"We say hello," Nell said, "and wish her a merry Christmas. And I say how sorry I am that Molly and Mick are going through a rough patch, especially at this time of the year."

Felicity sighed. "What a mess. I wish I could wave a magic wand and have everything go back to the way it used to be."

"Don't we all," Nell said, putting an arm around her daughter's shoulders. "But some things are just fine the way they are right now. We shouldn't forget that."

"I know, Mom," Felicity said. "I really do."

In spite of the frosty weather and the sometimes perilous walking conditions, the caroling had been an awful lot of fun. Mary Williams hadn't shown, and for a moment Nell had wondered if the thought of running into the Kings had put Mary off attending. More likely she had something else scheduled. Mrs. Williams was not one to be intimidated by awkward social situations or minor adversities. She was the sort who just got on with things.

As was Jill. She had joined the carolers, and though her voice was even worse than Molly's, it hadn't stopped her from singing at the top of her lungs. Nell and Felicity had stopped at Jill's house afterward. When Nell told her that Eric Manville would be joining them for Christmas dinner,

Jill had fetched the whiskey and added a celebratory shot to her cup of coffee and one to Nell's. "Let me know if you want me to bring mistletoe," she whispered when Felicity went off to the powder room. To which Nell had replied, "Jill, really!"

Now, tucked up in bed, Nell reached for the book of poetry Eric had given her earlier that day. She hadn't had a chance to open the volume before now and was surprised to find an inscription. *For Nell, whose words are as beautiful as her soul.* Eric's signature followed, the robust capital E, followed by the scrawl that represented the r, i, and c. Nell felt her heart leap. Surely it was the sentiment of a man in love? But, as she had thought before, perhaps a man in love with who she had been, not with whom she had become. Before Nell could puzzle out the message any further, her cell phone rang. It was Eric. With a smile, Nell answered.

"I'm back," Eric said. "Half frozen but back."

"How did it go?" Nell asked.

"Well, your cranberry crumble cookies were a big hit. At least three people asked for the recipe."

Nell snuggled down further under the covers. "But how did the reading go?"

"It went well," Eric told her. "But something odd happened afterward. A woman came up to tell me she had just found out about my divorce and was upset that the news had been kept quiet. She said she felt deceived."

"Oh. How did that make you feel?" Nell asked.

"It reminded me of how people feel so bonded with their favorite writers and musicians and actors. They feel we owe them not only attention but affection." Eric paused. "On the one hand, to know that you and your work means so much to a virtual stranger is humbling."

"Yes," Nell said. "I imagine it must be."

"On the other hand," Eric went on with a laugh, "it's kind of frightening. I'm just an ordinary guy. No one should be putting me on a pedestal, because I'm sure to fall right off!"

Nell laughed. "Your balance never has been good."

"Can't even ride a bicycle!"

"Did your fan ask for an apology?" Nell wondered.

"No," Eric said, "but I gave her one anyway. But enough about me. Have you had a chance to take a look at Gabrielle Lagum's poems?"

Nell touched the book by her side. "I'd just opened the cover when you called. All I've read so far is your inscription. It's lovely, Eric."

"I meant what I wrote."

"Thank you." Nell suddenly felt tongue-tied. Before words could come to her, Eric cleared his throat, and when he spoke his tone was light.

"About that cranberry crumble cookie recipe. I told your fans that I'd try to wrangle it out of you and pass it on. I hope you don't mind?"

"Of course not," Nell told him.

"I'll speak to you tomorrow?" he asked.

"Yes," Nell said. "Good night, Eric. I'm glad you called."

"Sleep well, Nell."

Nell set her cell phone on the bedside table and once again read the inscription Eric had written. Then with a smile she turned the page.

Chapter 32

"You're up early." Nell, sitting at the kitchen table with a cup of coffee and a half-eaten corn muffin, looked closely at her older daughter. There were dark circles under Molly's eyes and her face looked drawn.

"I've been awake since four," Molly said, slumping into the chair next to Nell's.

Nell noted that Molly was once again wearing the ring that had belonged to Mick's grandmother. For a moment she wondered if she should comment upon it and then decided not to say a word.

"Can I get you some breakfast?" she asked.

"No," Molly said. "That's okay. But I will have a cup of coffee."

Nell reached for the press pot and poured coffee into one of the mugs on the table. "Still no word from Mick?" she asked.

Molly shook her head. "Can I talk to you, Mom?"

"Of course," Nell said.

"Where do I even begin?" Molly took a sip of coffee before going on. "You know, it's ironic. I've been studying psychology for the past four years. You'd think I could have applied some of what I've learned to my own situation and *understood* myself better."

Nell patted her daughter's hand. "Self-knowledge is usually the most difficult to achieve. Don't punish yourself for being human."

"Not easy. Anyway, I've finally come to understand that for the past few months I've been terrified. And yet, I didn't *feel* afraid when I was going on about breaking up with Mick and seeing other men and leaving Yorktide behind. I felt brave. I didn't *know* I was afraid of what a life here in Maine with Mick represented until he started to give me those gifts, and then it all became so clear. I was *afraid*." Molly looked at the ring on her finger and shook her head. "Can fear tell you lies? I mean, can it make you believe your motives are good and healthy, like wanting to experience new things and meet new people, and not what they really are, which in my case was cowardice?"

"Yes," Nell said. "Fear can lie to you. It can make you do terrible things. It can lead you to make decisions against your own good." *Like walking away from Eric,* she thought. *Like turning my back on poetry.*

"I realize now," Molly went on, "that the depth of the love I feel for Mick frightened me. It didn't help that a lot of my friends thought I was nuts to want to get married to my first and only boyfriend." Molly smiled ruefully. "Some of them even congratulated me when I told them I'd broken up with Mick."

"I hope you realize that some of those critics might simply have been jealous of your relationship with Mick."

"I see that now." Molly paused for a moment before going on. "It's like, you graduate from college and you're supposed to start making adult decisions and living an adult life. For me, that meant marrying Mick like I'd planned. But suddenly, it felt as if everything was moving too fast. It felt as if the future was already here when I wasn't done with the present."

"And so deciding to move to Boston was a way to avoid making the most adult decision of all," Nell said.

"Exactly. To stay with someone I loved and who loved me. I want to be with Mick forever, Mom. I really do. I want to be an important part of his family and an important part of the farm."

"I know you do," Nell assured her. "And when you marry him I *know* you won't allow your true self to slip away, no matter how much a part of his family and the farm you become. Mick wouldn't want that, either. What you have with Mick is truly lovely."

Molly pulled her robe closer around her. "What I *had* with Mick. Now I have nothing."

Nell put her hand on her daughter's. "Don't be so sure," she said gently. "He needs time to heal. A young man's ego can be a very sensitive thing, and he'd put so much time and effort into making this Christmas special for you."

"I feel so ashamed, Mom," Molly confessed. "Sometimes I forget that men feel just as deeply as we do. What's wrong with me that I could ignore that fact?"

Nell wondered if Molly was thinking of her father as well as of Mick, but she refrained from asking. What she said was: "Don't be too hard on yourself, Molly. None of us are immune to fear. Sometimes it wins and sometimes it loses. I wish it lost all the time, but it doesn't."

Molly smiled wanly. "Thanks for listening, Mom. And thanks for trying to make me feel like less of a jerk. I really appreciate all you do for me."

I am needed, Nell thought. *I must never allow myself to forget that.* "It's my pleasure," she said honestly.

"So, what's the craft of the day?"

Nell sat back in her chair. In truth all she had planned

for the day other than preparing for tomorrow's Christmas dinner was to continue to read the book of poems Eric had given her. She laughed. "Nothing. I guess I'm finally out of ideas."

"There's still the window on the Advent calendar to open," Molly pointed out, getting up from the table. "December twenty-fourth," she said as she pulled open the last of the little cardboard windows of the big brick house. "It's a sprig of mistletoe." Molly turned to Nell. "Maybe it's a good omen."

"Maybe it is," Nell said. *Maybe it is for us both.*

Nell was sitting in the book nook of the living room when Eric called on her cell phone.

"Hi," he croaked.

"You don't sound very good," Nell said worriedly.

"I don't feel very good, either. I've got a cold coming on. But all I need is to stay in bed for the day. Works every time."

"I could bring you anything you need," Nell told him. "Cough medicine, aspirin, chicken soup."

"Don't go to any trouble, Nell. I'll be fine," he assured her.

"I was reading Gabrielle Lagum's poems when you called. Her work is really lovely. The poems are sharp and clear. They glitter with truth."

"I had a feeling her work would speak to you. I—" A cough interrupted Eric's next words.

"You should be trying to get some sleep," Nell told him. "You'll call me if you need anything, won't you?"

"I will, I promise. Thanks, Nell. I'm looking forward to tomorrow."

"Me too," she said. "Goodbye." In fact, it was only now that Nell realized just how much she was relying on Eric's being with her and the girls for Christmas. If he wasn't able to join them . . . The appearance of the girls turned Nell's thoughts away from the unhappy possibility.

Felicity went to the window that looked out onto the side yard. "I can't see anything but a wall of snow, not even the Masons' house, and that's only like twenty yards away. Isn't it awesome that no two snowflakes are identical," she said, turning to face the room.

Molly, still looking wan and pale, sank into the armchair across from her mother's. "You know, white is supposed to be the color of hope and purity and innocence, but sometimes it's scarier than black. Like today. The world looks so blanched and drained of life."

"In Chinese culture white is sometimes a symbol of death," Nell pointed out. "People wear white to funerals."

Felicity plopped onto the floor and sat cross-legged. "You two are depressing. What are you reading, Mom?"

"Eric gave me this book of poems by a young Ugandan writer."

Molly reached out for the book, and Nell passed it to her. She opened the book at the beginning and slowly turned a few pages. A moment later she returned it with a small smile. Nell realized that Molly must have seen Eric's inscription.

Felicity suddenly sprang up from the floor and pounded upstairs with no explanation.

"Does she ever sit still for long?" Nell asked rhetorically.

Molly rose from her chair. "Nope. I'll be back soon, Mom. I want to make one last delivery of goodies to the Pine Hill Residence for the Elderly before the weather gets any worse. And yes, Mom," she added with a smile, "I'll be careful."

Chapter 33

The weather was growing nastier by the minute. The windowpanes in the small mudroom at the back of the house were frosted inside and out. Snow laced the branches of the pine trees that marked the edge of the property and virtually obscured the stone birdbath in the center of the backyard. Nell was grateful for the blessing of her cozy home and hoped that Molly would be back before long. Molly was an excellent driver, but people rarely won when Mother Nature was the opponent.

Nell was in the living room admiring the decorations on the tree when the doorbell rang. She assumed it was the mailman with a package too big to slip through the mail slot or a Federal Express or UPS driver there to deliver something Felicity had ordered online. But when she opened the door she found her former husband instead.

"Joel!" she exclaimed. "This is a surprise. Come in."

Joel smiled. "Thanks. It's pretty nasty out here."

She took his black wool overcoat, hung it on the coat rack just inside the front door, and led him into the kitchen. She noticed that his perfectly trimmed hair was a bit grayer than it had been the last time she had seen him.

Otherwise he looked unchanged, the same tall, well built, ruggedly handsome man she had married so long ago. A college athlete who had never been sick a day in his life and for whom sartorial elegance was almost as necessary as breathing.

"I'm sorry to show up unannounced," Joel said.

"That's all right. But what could possibly bring you all the way from Cape Cod on a day like this?"

Joel blew on his hands to warm them before answering. "I've been feeling badly about Felicity's decision to cancel our plans to spend next Christmas together," he said. "She seemed so excited about the trip. I felt I had to see her face-to-face to be sure I haven't said something to put her off."

"And you thought if you surprised Felicity she wouldn't have time to put a mask in place if she really was upset with you."

"Something like that," Joel admitted, looking decidedly sheepish.

"Can I get you something to eat?" Nell asked.

"No, I had a bite along the way. But a cup of coffee would be welcome if it's no trouble."

"None at all." Nell put the kettle on to boil and measured ground coffee into the French press pot. "I admit I was totally surprised when Fliss changed her mind about spending Christmas abroad."

"So, you didn't say anything to influence her decision?" Joel asked.

"Joel, you know me," Nell scolded. "I would never try to keep your children from you or you from your children. I hate the fact that Molly won't have anything to do with you, and she knows I hate it."

"I'm sorry. It's just that Fliss's about-face came out of the blue."

Nell handed him a cup of coffee. "Still take it black?" she asked.

Joel accepted the cup. "Yeah, thanks. So, is Fliss around?"

"Yes. She's upstairs."

"Good. I can't stay long. I've got to be back before Taylor goes to bed. Pam feels we should both be there every night at bedtime to read him stories."

Nell recalled how little Joel had participated in the day-to-day parenting of their girls, but then again, his absences had never bothered her. She had enjoyed her role as the primary parent, never fussing when Joel stayed late at the office or missed a school play or soccer game for a round of golf or an evening of cocktails with his colleagues and clients. In hindsight her complaisance and satisfaction seemed naïve. Pam Bertrand was a very different woman, Nell reflected, someone quite sure of her place in the world outside the home. Maybe living with such a woman was doing Joel's character some good.

"Is Taylor's father still giving you and Pam a hard time about the custody agreement?" Nell asked.

"The situation has not improved," Joel replied grimly. "The man has some sort of perverse need to cause trouble. The moment one issue is settled he's back with another."

"Is Taylor aware of what's been going on?" Nell asked.

"Yes, unfortunately, though his mother and I try to shield him as best we can. But I didn't come to Yorktide to talk about Pam and Taylor." Joel lowered his voice. "How's Molly? Is she at home?"

"She's out delivering cookies to our local home for the elderly. Joel, she did indeed break up with Mick, and it was ugly. Now she bitterly regrets her decision. You were right. It was a bad case of cold feet. The problem is that

Mick won't talk to her. She's afraid she's lost him for good."

Joel shook his head. "I just assumed Molly wanted to stretch her wings a bit before coming back to Yorktide and marrying. I didn't know she was so confused. Well, of course I didn't. She hasn't talked to me in three years."

"Dad!" Felicity was standing in the doorway of the kitchen. "What a surprise." She gave her father a hug, which he returned carefully as he was still holding his coffee. "Is everything okay? Are Pam and Taylor with you?"

"No, they're home on the Cape," Joel explained. "I had to see you, Fliss. I had to be sure I didn't do or say anything to put you off wanting to spend next Christmas with the three of us."

Felicity laughed. "But I already told you that you had nothing to do with my decision! I just want to spend Christmas at home. I have such happy memories of holidays in this house. But hey, if you want to take me to Europe some other time, Dad, you can. There's always spring break. They say nothing beats April in Paris."

Joel smiled. "Okay, I believe you. I'd see it in your eyes if you were lying. And April in Paris *is* pretty great." Joel turned to Nell. "Your mom and I spent a wonderful week in the City of Lights before Molly was born. Remember?"

Nell smiled. "How could I forget?"

"Did Taylor get the package I sent him?" Felicity asked.

Joel put his empty cup on the counter and smiled. "He did. And he's beyond excited to see what Santa and his elves are bringing him tomorrow."

"Good. Give him and Pam a big kiss for me." Felicity suddenly pulled her phone from her pocket. "Yikes. I have a Skype session with Amanda in like two minutes."

"The girl who used to live next door when you were little?" Joel asked.

"Yeah. We've kept in touch." With another hug and wishes for a happy Christmas, Felicity was off, pounding up the stairs to her room.

"Where does she get her energy?" Joel asked with a smile.

Nell laughed. "Sugar." Just then she heard the front door open and shut and her heart leapt to her throat. Joel shot her a nervous look. It could only be Molly.

"Whose car is that in the drive?" Molly asked, entering the kitchen a moment later. She came to an abrupt halt when she saw her father. "Oh. It's you. What are you doing here?"

Nell saw her ex-husband swallow hard before replying. "Merry Christmas, Molly," he said. "I've missed you."

Nell felt her shoulders tense. She had absolutely no idea what Molly would do or say. But before Nell could speculate, Molly launched herself into her father's arms and burst out crying.

Joel held Molly tight and stroked her head. "It's all right," he whispered. "It's okay."

Nell felt tears prick her eyes, and she clasped her hands to her chest.

After a moment or two, Molly stepped away from her father, and Nell hurried to give her a tissue with which to mop her eyes. "I've missed you too, Dad," Molly said thickly. "I'm sorry for pushing you away. It was wrong."

"You were angry with me," Joel said quietly. "You felt you needed the distance."

"You don't have to make excuses for me," she countered. "I acted like a self-centered child, and I'm sorry for it."

Joel smiled. "Okay," he said. "I accept your apology.

And I'm sorry for . . . I could have handled things better six years ago."

"But it was six years ago," Molly said. "We can't change the past. Now is what's important. And I don't want to be mad anymore. It's stupid. It's a waste of time."

"I'm glad to hear that. Really glad."

Molly smiled tentatively. "Please wish Pam and Taylor a merry Christmas from me. I know I haven't been great about acknowledging either of them, but that will change, I promise."

Joel nodded. "I'll tell them both you send Christmas wishes." Joel looked at his watch. "I'd better get going," he said. "It's going to be a long trip back to the Cape."

"You're driving home today?" Molly asked.

"That's my plan, yes."

Molly looked quickly at her mother. "Dad," she said, "maybe you should stay. The roads are dangerous. They're talking about whiteout conditions in places."

"I'll be okay," Joel assured her. "Don't worry."

"If you're sure." Molly gave her father another hug. "I'll let you two say goodbye in private. Let's talk soon, Dad."

Nell watched as her older daughter left the room, and then she glanced out the window at the snow falling thick and heavy. "Molly's right, Joel," she said. "I don't think you should drive back to the Cape. I can make up the couch in the living room. You can spend Christmas morning with us, and head out after breakfast if the weather improves. I'm sure Pam will understand."

Joel shook his head. "I couldn't intrude."

"You wouldn't be intruding. We're having other guests tomorrow, too. My friend Jill is joining us." Nell hesitated a moment and then went on. "And do you remember my old friend from college, Eric Manville?"

"The writer?" Joel asked.

"Yes. He's staying in Ogunquit for a few weeks, and I invited him for Christmas dinner."

"Pam will be green with envy. She loves his books. So you two have been in touch?"

"Only recently," Nell explained. "He did a reading in town and I went. We've met a few times since then."

Joel looked at Nell searchingly. "Did he come here just to see you?" he asked. "It seems an odd time of the year for a big-name author like Eric Manville to be giving a reading in sleepy little Yorktide."

Nell met her ex-husband's gaze steadily. "No," she said. "It was just a coincidence. Eric had no idea I lived in Yorktide. Besides, he's been doing other appearances and readings around Southern Maine."

Joel nodded and cleared his throat. "Thanks, Nell, but I'll take my chances. If things get really bad I'll pull over somewhere and wait out the storm. I've got blankets and flares and a six-pack of water. I'll be fine."

"All right," she said. "If you're sure. But promise to let me know when you're back safely on the Cape."

"I promise. Nell, I'm glad I came today. And I'm happy to see you well."

"I'm glad you came, too," Nell said. "What just happened between you and Molly was wonderful."

"It was, and I so hope we can reclaim the good relationship we had before the divorce. I'm certainly going to try my best to make amends." Joel smiled. "Maybe this year she'll actually deposit her Christmas check from me and not just tear it up."

Together Nell and Joel walked to the front hall. "Will you be seeing your father this Christmas?" Nell asked.

Joel shook his head. "Doubtful," he said. "We invited

him and his wife to a small cocktail party we gave last week, and neither bothered to reply. What about your parents? Are they well?"

"Your guess is as good as mine. I'm not sure they'd bother to tell me if they weren't. I'll call them tomorrow and we'll exchange a few pleasantries and that will be that until the next holiday."

Joel sighed. "It's strange how things turn out, isn't it?"

"Strange isn't the word."

"It looks like you've gone all out with the decorations this year," Joel said as they passed through the dining room and then into the living room. "Is that another tree I see on the landing?"

Nell laughed. "It is. I'm afraid I've become Christmas crazed."

"There are worse things to be. Nell, you've done a fine job with our daughters. Thank you."

"You were involved in their upbringing, too," Nell pointed out.

"Not like you were. Not like you still are."

When they reached the front door, Joel put on his coat and then laid his hand lightly on Nell's shoulder. "Nell, do you ever wonder . . . I mean, sometimes I think that I—"

"Joel," Nell said, gently removing his hand. "Please. Don't say anything more. What's done is done."

"All right. Take care of yourself, Nell."

Nell opened the door and watched as Joel, head bowed against the swirling snow, made his way to his car. Only when his vehicle was out of sight did she go back into the house and close the door behind her. Molly and Felicity were waiting for her in the kitchen.

"I thought you were talking to Amanda," Nell said.

"The Internet is down," Felicity explained. "Must be the storm."

"Did you tell your sister what happened between you and your father?" Nell asked her older daughter as she took a seat at the table.

Molly nodded. Her eyes were still red from crying. "Yes."

"You really had no idea Dad would be coming today?" Felicity asked her mother.

"None. Molly and I both suggested he stay because of the bad weather, but he seemed determined to get back. I told him to let me know when he gets home safely."

Felicity shook her head. "I'm sorry he came all this way just to make sure I was okay."

"What do you mean?" Molly asked.

"Dad was worried he'd said or done something to put me off going with him and Pam and Taylor to Switzerland next year," Felicity explained. "He said he wanted to see me in person to be sure I wasn't upset. Dad's a good guy. I'm so glad you made up with him, Molly."

Molly sank into a seat at the table and wiped a stray tear from her cheek. "It was weird," she said. "The moment I saw Dad standing next to you, Mom, it became clear to me that I was wrong. What was I hoping to accomplish by avoiding Dad these past few years? I can't turn back time and make him stay with us. I've been so mean to him, and yet he was still nice enough to offer to help me out when I said I was moving to Boston."

"He loves you, Molly," Nell said. "He loves us all."

"I know. The least I can do is to give him a chance. He's not perfect, but no one is. I'm certainly not, and Mick would be the first to agree."

"I have a good feeling about you two," Felicity said robustly. "Christmas can be a magical time. Just try to believe, okay? Look at what just happened with you and Dad. Like the song says, let your heart be light."

Nell put her arm around Molly's shoulders. "Your sister is right. Don't lose faith in miracles."

"Do you really believe in miracles, Mom?" Molly asked with a wobbly smile.

"You know," Nell said, "I think that I do."

Chapter 34

Nell had prepared a simple meal of pasta with sausage and broccoli and tomato sauce she had made at the end of the tomato harvest back in September. As she set the kitchen table, she thought about the call she had made to Eric late that afternoon. He swore he was feeling much better and that nothing would keep him from joining the King family for Christmas. Nell smiled as she placed a fork by her plate. This Christmas was not turning out to be the quiet, private little holiday she had wanted it to be. She had gone into the season with expectations for one reality and now she was facing another, maybe even a better reality. *Resiliency and optimism,* Nell thought as she placed the last napkin on the table. *Both were awfully useful tools to have in one's hand.*

The girls came into the kitchen then. "Just in time," Nell said, as she brought a large bowl of the pasta to the table.

Felicity dropped into her chair, singing in her pretty soprano voice. " '*Later on we'll conspire, as we dream by the fire, to face unafraid the plans that we made, walking in a winter wonderland.*' Remember when I was an elf in my second grade Christmas play," she asked suddenly, "and I fell on stage because of those stupid elf boots? The toes were like a mile long."

Molly smiled. "What I remember most was how you just picked yourself up and got on with things. When that little boy fell over the toes of *his* elf boots, he made such a howling racket!"

"That was Curtis Murray. His family moved to Portland when we were in sixth grade. I wonder if he's still a drama queen."

"I remember the Murrays. There was an older son who went to school with Mick." Molly sighed. "I can't help but wonder what Mick planned on bringing me today. Do you know his mother told me that when he was only ten he bought her a Byers' Choice collectible figure for Christmas. He saved every penny of the money he'd made from his paper route and from shoveling snow and raking leaves for that old couple that used to own Spiny Ridge Farm. He's always been so thoughtful and selfless." Molly turned to Nell. "Mom? Do you think he was planning to propose tomorrow?"

Nell sighed. "Oh, Molly, I don't know."

"Try not to think about it," Felicity said. "Think about something else, like the fact that a famous writer is spending Christmas with us!"

"Are you nervous about Eric's being here tomorrow?" Molly asked.

"Why would she be nervous?" Felicity asked. "They're friends."

"They were more than that, once," Molly said quietly. "And you know what they say about first loves."

Nell reached for Molly's hand. "That you never forget them."

"Hey, you two," Felicity said brightly. "I have an idea.

Why don't we go to church in the morning? I know we haven't gone in a long time, but somehow this year it feels like the right thing to do."

Molly nodded. "I'm in. A little prayer never hurt anybody."

"I think going to church is a great idea," Nell said. "A really great idea."

Home safely. Merry Xmas.

Nell read Joel's text with a sense of relief and returned to wrapping the final present. She had decided to give Molly her great aunt Prudence's serving platter after all; there really was no reason not to. Once the platter was wrapped, the duties Nell had set herself this Christmas season would be done. The stockings were completed; the craft materials were put away; the baking supplies were stowed in cupboards. All that was left now was to enjoy every moment of Christmas Day with her family. And with her friends.

Nell affixed a final piece of tape to the package with a sigh of satisfaction. She felt calm and yet strangely excited. She put the package aside, went to the window, and leaned close to the pane. The scene she saw was odd, a strange play of light from the room behind her, darkness beyond, gray swaths in between. She remembered how Molly had said that white could be a more frightening color than black; she had said that the snow-covered world looked blanched and drained of life. An image began to form somewhere inside Nell, and she felt a strange fluttering throughout her body.

Abruptly, Nell turned from the window and hurried over to her desk. She reached for a pen and one of her old notebooks from the pile stacked atop the desk. She opened the notebook, and along a clean margin she began to write, her thoughts outdistancing her hand. She frowned and crossed out a word and scribbled three more, turning the notebook to follow the clean margin. She wrote until suddenly she stopped. She read what she had written and nodded. The resulting lines were perhaps not very good, but what was good was that the impulse, the *need* to write had returned. Nell laughed to herself. She would need to buy some new notebooks and a package of her favorite blue pens and maybe the good old-fashioned number two pencils she had loved to use. And a pencil sharpener. She would need a pencil sharpener, too.

Nell closed the curtains over the window, got into bed, and turned off the lamp on her bedside table. She knew now for a fact that even if tomorrow proved to be the last time she ever saw Eric Manville face-to-face, she would be okay. For an unbelievable second time in her life he had gifted her with energy and belief in her talents. And she was stronger now than she had been all those years ago, strong enough to finally live as she had been meant to live, with poetry in her soul. And with poetry in her soul she would never truly be alone.

Molly was right, Nell thought, her eyes beginning to close. *You never did forget your first love.* For some that could be a curse, but for Nell it had turned out to be a blessing.

Chapter 35

The sun shone brightly Christmas morning, almost blindingly so. Snow was no longer falling from the sky but was heaped fantastically on every surface, from the ground to the birdbath, from the branches of trees to the outcropping of rock along the left side of the backyard. Earlier, Nell had spotted a cardinal swooping across the front yard, a pop of scarlet that brought a smile to her face.

The King family was gathered around the kitchen table. Nell had made eggs Benedict for all three of them; the girls had long ago lost interest in pancakes shaped like angels.

"I am so going to miss your cooking when I'm away at school next year," Felicity stated. "You're going to send me care packages, right?"

Nell smiled. "Sure, but I don't think eggs Benedict will travel well."

Felicity was wearing the white gold and diamond cocktail ring that had belonged to her great aunt Prudence. It didn't quite go with her plaid pajamas and fuzzy robe, but Felicity didn't seem to mind. Molly had thanked her mother sincerely for the gift of the platter; Nell believed it would get good and frequent use wherever and with whomever her daughter established her own home.

Felicity suddenly dropped her fork on the table, sat back in her chair, and groaned. "I don't think I can eat another bite all day after that breakfast."

"Haven't you ever heard of pacing yourself?" Molly asked with a smile.

Felicity groaned again. "Apparently not."

"Shoveling will make you hungry again. We at least need to clear the driveway and the path to the front door." Molly suddenly rose from the table. "Let's go into the living room," she said. "Fliss and I have one more present for you, Mom."

"Like the sweater from L. L. Bean and the new leather gloves from the Bass outlet weren't enough? Really, you shouldn't have spent so much money on me."

Felicity reached for her mother's hand and pulled her up from her seat. "Just come on," she said.

When they were in the living room, Molly directed her mother to the center of the couch and sat on her left. Felicity retrieved a package about the size of a trade paperback book from a drawer in the credenza and sat on her mother's right.

"Go ahead," she said. "Open it."

"What are you two up to?" Nell asked as she carefully peeled back the wrapping paper to reveal a framed photograph of two smiling young women, each perched on one knee of a man in a Santa Claus costume. The young women were Molly and Felicity King. They were wearing elf hats. Molly wore a red sweater and a silver brooch in the shape of a snowflake. Felicity wore a green scarf and a brooch in the shape of a reindeer.

Tears sprang to Nell's eyes. "This photo means everything to me," she said. "*Everything.*"

"Good," Molly told her, "because not everyone at Santa Central was happy about us wanting to sit on Santa's lap. The mall guard told us it was just for children and that we had to leave, so I told him that Fliss and I *were* children and that we were having the picture taken for our mother as a surprise and if he didn't let us on line he would be ruining a woman's Christmas." Molly grinned. "I might have hinted that you were sick and that this might be your last Christmas."

Nell laughed and wiped a few remaining tears from her cheeks.

"Anyway, it was Fliss's idea to get the picture taken," Molly explained. "I wasn't sure about it at first, but I'm glad we did it."

"Me, too." Nell put an arm around each of her daughters. "I was so focused on this Christmas possibly being our last together I almost forgot that we're all here together *now,* and this moment in time is what counts the most."

"Our last Christmas together?" Felicity said. "What are you talking about, Mom? Even if we move to California or London or wherever we'll always come home to Yorktide and to you. Why wouldn't we? You've been an awesome mother and a great role model."

"Even though I never had a big exciting career?" Nell asked.

Molly laughed. "Nothing against having a big exciting career, but what kid wouldn't prefer to come home to her mother after school rather than to an empty house? You did fine, Mom. What matters in the end is how much a child is loved."

"I agree!" Felicity reached for the heavily decorated brown paper that had been wrapped around one of the presents Nell had given her. "And I'd say that anyone who takes the time to put together this amazing gift paper instead of just buying a cheap roll of shiny stuff at the grocery store has a lot of love to give her kids."

"You're okay with the fact that I didn't get you the designer bag you wanted?" Nell asked.

"Yeah. It was crazy expensive. I don't know what I was thinking. This Christmas is perfect just the way it is."

"Except maybe for the stockings," Molly said with a smile, pointing to Nell's creations that were sitting under the tree in a lump.

"I think they're . . . nice," Felicity said lamely.

Nell laughed. "No they're not. They're awful. I can't knit to save my life. You guys were right in teasing me about my going overboard this Christmas. The pomander balls, the baking, the crèche, the trees, the Advent calendar . . . I was trying to prove that nothing out there in the big wide world is better than what you have here at home."

"Mom," Felicity said with mock seriousness, "you're kind of a nut, you know that?"

Molly gave her mother a one-armed hug. "But you're our nut and we love you."

"Thanks. I'll miss you girls when you move on. But that's okay. I want you to grow and live and love. I want you to accomplish every little thing you want to accomplish. Just do me a favor, and tell me all about it."

"Every little thing?" Felicity asked teasingly.

"Okay, maybe not everything. Just the stuff that won't cause a heart attack."

Nell felt a deep sense of contentment as she sat on the couch between her daughters this Christmas morning. She knew for sure now that the nest would never truly be empty. Her children would never abandon her, just as she would never abandon them. Eric was right when he said that a parent never ceases to be a parent. That awful phrase "post-parental" was just wrong.

And now that she had welcomed poetry back into her life, she had yet another purpose to give her days meaning. "I've decided to sign up for a poetry course at YCC," Nell announced. "It's my Christmas present to myself."

Felicity nodded. "Way to go, Mom."

"I guess we should call Grandma and Grandpa Emerson," Molly noted suddenly.

"Let's not mention the fact that Eric Manville will be joining us for Christmas dinner," Nell advised. "I suspect that information might elicit a response that won't fit well with the spirit of the season."

Nell took her cell phone from the pocket of her robe, punched in her parents' number, and switched to speaker-phone mode. Her mother answered after three rings. "Merry Christmas," Nell, Molly, and Felicity chorused.

"Oh," Jacqueline Emerson replied after a moment. "And to you."

"Is Dad there?" Nell asked.

"Tal is out playing golf," her mother informed them.

"What are you two doing for Christmas?" Felicity asked.

Jacqueline told them that they were having dinner with another couple at the best restaurant in town. "The wine list is renowned," she said. "Nell, you never knew much about wine, did you?"

"No, Mom," Nell said evenly. "I didn't and I still don't."

The conversation went on in a desultory manner for a few moments before Jacqueline Emerson ended the call.

"You know," Felicity said, "I don't think Grandma is a happy person."

"Not that she'd ever say anything to us about her feelings," Molly added.

"I think you might be right, Fliss," Nell said. She could remember very few occasions on which her mother had genuinely smiled, let alone laughed. Suddenly she felt a surge of sympathy for Jacqueline Emerson.

The miniature grandfather clock chiming the half hour interrupted Nell's thoughts. "We'd better get moving or we'll be late for the service," she said, rising from the couch.

"How many years has it been since we went to church on Christmas?" Molly asked.

"Too many," Nell replied. "Too many."

Chapter 36

"That's him!" Felicity dashed from the kitchen. Nell took a deep breath and followed more slowly. She had only reached the entrance to the living room when Felicity flung open the door to admit Eric Manville.

"Hi!" Felicity cried. "Hi!"

"You might want to ask him in." Molly, who had been sitting on the couch with a book, joined her sister at the door.

Felicity stepped back hurriedly. "Right, come in!"

Eric did. Molly extended her hand. "I'm Molly," she said. "And the person jumping around behind me is Felicity."

"This is just so exciting," Felicity said, extending her hand as well.

Nell smiled fondly. Eric was wearing his puffer coat and that awful green hat. "I told you they were fans," she said. "How are you feeling?"

"Right as rain," Eric said. "I forgot to ask what I could bring, but I figured I couldn't go wrong with champagne and chocolate."

Molly relieved Eric of his coat and hat and then accepted the gift bag from which two champagne bottles peeked. Felicity accepted the box of candy wrapped in gold paper and tied with a green ribbon.

Eric looked from the massive tree to the crèche, from the gingerbread house to the row of candles on the mantel of the fireplace, from the bowl of ribbon candy to the garland decorating the handrail of the stairs. "Wow," he said. "It's like a winter wonderland in here."

Felicity laughed. "Or like a specialty Christmas shop exploded! Mom went a little crazy with the decorations this year. And with the baking. I think a few of my teeth have rotted out."

"She mentioned the baking," Eric told her. "Maybe I shouldn't have brought chocolates."

"No!" Felicity cried, hugging the box to her chest.

"Is it totally not okay to ask you to autograph my copy of *The Land of Joy*?" Molly requested.

"It totally *is* okay," Eric assured her.

The doorbell sounded again. This time it was Jill, bearing a promised bowl of mashed potatoes and turnips and a green-bean-with-almonds casserole. After Nell had eased her friend of her burdens, she introduced her to Eric.

"I saw you the other evening at the Bookworm," Eric noted as he shook Jill's hand. "You were sitting with Nell."

"That's right. I'm a fan of your work."

"Thank you. I—"

"Hey, Eric," Felicity interrupted. "Do you want to help me make the gravy?"

"He's a guest, Fliss," Molly pointed out. "He's here to enjoy himself."

"I'm happy to help in any way I can," Eric said. "Lead on." After taking Jill's contributions from Nell, Eric followed Felicity to the kitchen.

"Well, Felicity already seems to consider him part of the

family," Jill whispered. Before Nell could reply, the doorbell rang for a third time.

"I'll get it." Molly hurried to the front door. Nell was sure her daughter was hoping the visitor would be Mick, but when Molly opened the door it was to find Stuart Smith standing on the welcome mat. With his wool beanie and big brown beard he looked a bit like Yukon Cornelius, prospector and friend of the Abominable Snowman.

"Please tell me my mother is here," he said. "I went to her place, and when I found it empty I got a little freaked."

"Hey, Stuart. Come in, she's here."

Stuart strode toward his mother and embraced her.

"What on earth are you doing here?" Jill cried. "Never mind, you're here and that's all that matters."

When Stuart finally let his mother go, he held out the bag he was carrying. "I brought a cheese ball."

Nell relieved him of his package and gave him a kiss on the cheek. "Hello, Stuart. It's good to see you."

"How did you get through?" Jill asked. "The news reports say that a big stretch of Route One is closed."

"With difficulty." Stuart took his mother's hand in his. "I'm sorry, Mom. I shouldn't have made other plans when I know spending Christmas together means so much to you—and to me. Especially this first Christmas without Brian."

Jill nodded. "Thank you, Stuart. So, what's become of the girlfriend? Sherry? Brandy? Whiskey?"

"Taffy. I gave her the airline tickets and she went off with a friend. I don't think I'll be seeing her again. But that's okay. It was nothing serious. I shouldn't have been wasting my time or hers." Stuart turned to Nell. "So, is it okay if I join you for dinner?"

"Of course," Nell told him. "The more the merrier."

"I'm grateful for your hospitality. And frankly, I could

use a home-cooked meal. I'm useless in the kitchen, and the women I date don't seem to have any interest in feeding me."

Jill patted her son's arm. "You should let me pick your next lady friend."

Stuart sighed. "I might take you up on that offer, Mom. I don't seem to be doing very well on my own."

Eric suddenly came into the living room, Felicity closely trailing behind. He was wearing one of the aprons Nell had bought for the girls. "What's all the excitement?" he asked.

"Eric," Nell said, restraining a laugh at the sight of the apron and the smudge of flour on Eric's cheek. "This is Jill's son, Stuart."

Eric came forward and extended his hand. "Eric Manville. Nice to meet you."

"*The* Eric Manville?" Stuart asked, giving Eric's hand a shake.

"If by that you mean am I the one who writes books, yeah, that's me."

"Wow," Stuart said. "I don't think I've ever met a famous writer in person before."

"As you can see we're pretty unremarkable in the flesh. Except for when we're wearing aprons decorated with bunnies and foxes. I was working on the gravy."

"Stuart brought a cheese ball," Nell told Eric, whose eyes lit up at the news.

"Good man. So, where is it?"

Jill laughed. "I'll put it out and pop open a bottle of champagne."

Everyone followed Jill to the kitchen, where Stuart offered to take on any chore Nell set him to; Molly leaned against a counter and stared down at her phone, no doubt in the hope that Mick was reaching out to her; and Felicity chatted with Eric as he continued to work on the gravy. Nell smiled as she watched them all. She wondered what other miracles could possibly be in store for them this Christmas Day. *Please God,* she thought. *Let it be the miracle Molly is praying for.*

Chapter 37

Molly's air of melancholy had deepened as the afternoon progressed. Just before dinner Nell found her standing at the living room window, looking out at not much of anything but the darkening day. Nell went over to her and put an arm around her shoulder. "You okay?" she whispered.

"Not really," Molly said with a wan smile. "But please don't let me spoil this day for you, Mom."

"It's time for dinner. Come with me."

Molly linked her arm through Nell's, and together they went into the dining room where the others were gathered. The table was set with the Waterford crystal and the Lennox dinnerware Nell had so rarely used since her divorce. Linen napkins replaced the paper ones the King family used on a daily basis, and two white tapers stood tall in silver candlesticks.

"Everything looks delicious!" Felicity said, clasping her hands before her. "My appetite is totally back."

The group took their seats, Nell at one end of the table and Jill at the other. Eric and Molly sat across from Stuart and Felicity. Nell had carved the turkey in the kitchen and now helped her guests to legs or breast meat and gravy. In addition to Jill's mashed potatoes with turnips and green beans with almonds, there was sausage and mushroom stuffing, chunky cranberry sauce, and hot homemade rolls. Within a few minutes plates were piled high and glasses were filled. Just as Nell was about to suggest a toast, the doorbell rang for the fourth time that day.

Molly leapt from her seat. "I'll get it," she said, hurrying from the dining room.

"Could it be?" Jill said, looking to Nell.

"I know I shouldn't but . . ." Nell got up from the table and tiptoed to the little hall between the dining and living room, from where she had a view of the front door. She was just in time to see Molly open the door to Mick Williams.

"I brought a present from my mother," he said without preamble. "She knows how your mother loves her fruit-cake."

Without a word Molly threw herself into his arms. Mick held her tightly, narrowly avoiding dropping the fruitcake onto the floor.

"Who's that?" Stuart whispered, and Nell jumped. She hadn't noticed that everyone had followed her and were also witnesses to the scene.

"Molly's boyfriend," Jill told him softly.

"I knew it," Felicity whispered. "Christmas magic."

"I didn't mean what I said!" Molly cried. "I *do* love you, Mick! I love you with all my heart. I've been so confused and scared, but I want to tell you everything I've been thinking and make it all right."

Though Nell couldn't see Mick's face as he took Molly's hand, she was sure it beamed with pleasure and relief. "Good," he said. "Because together I know we can solve any problem we run up against." Suddenly, Mick looked down at Molly's hand in his. "You're wearing my grand-mother's ring."

"Oh," Molly said. "I'm sorry. I—"

"I *want* you to have it, Molly. It's what I've always wanted."

"Thank you," she whispered.

"My mom expects me back for dinner, but why don't I come by after. We can talk."

Molly nodded. "I'd like that, Mick."

"He's leaving!" Jill hissed. "Hurry!"

Nell and the others scooted back to their seats in the dining room. Stuart's chair scraped the floor as he sat and he mouthed "Sorry." Eric held his fork and knife aloft as if about to dig into his meal. Jill's fixed smile looked more like a rictus of death. Felicity began to whistle under her breath. Nell folded her arms across her chest, then un-folded then, then folded her hands on the table.

A moment later Molly was standing in the doorway to the dining room. Her eyes sparkled and her cheeks were flushed, not only, Nell guessed, from the cold air that had come in along with Mick.

"Who was it?" Felicity asked, widening her eyes in a ridiculous attempt to look innocent.

"You know very well who it was," Molly said. "Do you think I didn't hear you all whispering behind me? And I'm sure Mick could see you!"

Nell unfolded her hands and put them on her lap. "Sorry, Molly. We didn't mean to—"

"Yes, you did, and it's fine, really. I'm so happy right now I could burst!"

"Don't do that," Nell instructed. "Sit and eat."

Molly dropped into her seat next to Eric. "I'm suddenly ravenous!"

"Didn't I tell you to believe in miracles?" Felicity said to her sister.

"You did," Molly admitted, "but it's not always easy."

"I think it's time for a toast," Nell announced.

Eric raised his glass. "To Christmas in Maine!"

Next, Jill raised her glass. "To Christmas with the three Kings!"

"To being *home* for Christmas!" Felicity proclaimed.

Stuart looked to Jill. "To my mother, to whom I owe every good thing in my life."

"To my friends and family," Molly said, "who helped me survive these last horrible days. Your turn, Mom."

"To an absolutely perfect Christmas," Nell announced. "Cheers!"

Chapter 38

It was nine o'clock on Christmas night. Jill and Stuart had gone home laden with leftovers. Felicity was watching a movie in her bedroom. Mick had come by for Molly as promised. Eric and Nell were standing in front of the tree in the living room; it was the first time they had been alone all day. The fire in the grate was still crackling away. The aroma of fresh pine mixed with the lingering scents of warm apple and pumpkin pie. Nell had never felt so utterly content as she did at that moment.

Eric nodded toward the picture of Molly and Felicity with Santa Claus that had pride of place on the mantel. "That picture is worth a thousand words," he said.

"I think it's the best gift I've ever gotten from my children," Nell told him. "But there was another wonderful gift as well. Joel made a surprise visit yesterday. He wanted to be sure he hadn't done or said anything to make Felicity change her mind about spending next Christmas with him in Switzerland. She assured him that he was innocent. But the best thing about the visit was that Molly and her father reconciled."

"You're right," Eric agreed. "Reconciliation is a pretty wonderful Christmas gift."

Nell smiled up at him. "And you're being here with me and the girls is also a gift."

"As it is for me as well." Eric suddenly reached into his jacket pocket, took out a folded piece of paper, and handed it to Nell. "Here," he said.

Nell took the paper, unfolded it, and scanned the few lines written in dark blue ink. It was a moment before her mind registered what it was she was reading.

"I wrote this," she said, looking back to Eric in wonder. "I wrote this for you."

"I know." Eric enfolded her hands in his and held them to his chest. "I've kept everything you ever wrote for me," he said softly. "Your poems, your letters, even little notes. Nell, I have something to confess. I asked my publisher to schedule the reading at the Bookworm specifically because I knew you lived in Yorktide. I wanted to see you again."

Nell shook her head. "Why now?"

"It was something I've wanted to do for a long time," Eric admitted, "but I suppose I had to work up the courage first. There was always the chance you wouldn't want anything to do with me. There was always the chance that you were still happily married with no time for reminiscing with a former boyfriend."

"What if I hadn't come to the reading?" Nell asked. Her heart was pounding so hard now she could barely hear her own words over the sound of it.

"I would have sought you out. Nell," Eric went on, "you know I've never been good at doing things the way they probably should be done, but so much time has been wasted and you're *not* married any longer and . . . The thing is, I'm still in love with you."

"Oh, Eric," Nell breathed. "I'm still in love with you, too."

A smile of delight broke out across his face. "Maybe

this sounds corny, but I believe it was fate that brought us together in the first place and fate that brought us back to each other after all these years."

"Not corny," Nell told him. "Beautiful."

Eric clasped her hands more tightly. "Look, here I go jumping the gun again, but I don't want to be apart from you any longer. What I'd like is to move to Yorktide, but only if it's what you would like. After all, I can write from anywhere, and besides, I'm tired of New York. What do you think?" he asked.

"I think," Nell said, tears brimming in her eyes, "that I would like that very much. A leap of faith on my part is long overdue."

And then their lips met in a kiss Nell realized she had been waiting and hoping for since the last time she had laid eyes on Eric all those years ago. Finally, after what seemed like both an eternity and an instant, they drew apart. Nell took Eric's hand and led him to the couch, where they sat curled together, Eric's arm around her shoulder, her hand clasped in his.

"I was so worried you wouldn't feel the way I do," Eric said softly. "Revisiting the past is risky."

"But sometimes you have no choice. When I saw you at the Bookworm that night . . ." Nell shook her head. "I was so scared to be there, but I just couldn't stay away."

"You *did* have a choice, Nell. And you chose to be brave."

"All right," Nell agreed with a smile. "I chose to be brave. And it was worth the risk."

"Do you think the girls will be okay with our being together?" Eric asked.

"I do," Nell said. "They're pretty amazing people. And Eric? I managed to write a few lines of poetry last night.

They're not great," she added quickly, "but they're not terrible, either. And I'm signing up for a poetry course at the community college."

"That's fantastic news, Nell," Eric said. "Very little could make me happier. Will you allow me to read your work as it progresses?"

"Yes. It's the least I can do to show my appreciation for what you've done for me this Christmas."

Eric laughed a bit embarrassedly. "What have I done other than deceive you about why I came to Yorktide?"

"You've given me the gift of myself," Nell told him earnestly.

Eric gently pressed his lips to her forehead. "You had yourself all along. Maybe I just reminded you it was there."

"Either way, I want you to be honest in your criticism of my work like you were back in the old days. Here," Nell said, returning the piece of paper on which so long ago she had written a poem for Eric. "It was meant for you."

"Thank you. Wait, I almost forgot. I have something else to show you." Eric took an envelope from the same jacket pocket in which he had stowed the poem and handed it to Nell. She opened the envelope and withdrew a four-by-six-inch photograph. It was the photo she so ardently wished she still possessed.

"This has always been my favorite picture of the two of us," Eric told her.

Nell wiped a tear from her eye. "Mine, too. In fact, I thought about asking if you remembered this day. I felt sick when my mother told me she had thrown away a box of my things that included this picture." Gently Nell put her hand against Eric's cheek. "But now I have you in the flesh, not just in my mind's eye."

They kissed again, and it was with greater reluctance

than each had felt a few moments earlier that their lips finally parted.

"I should go," Eric said. "I'm thinking you and the girls have a lot to talk about."

They made plans to meet the following morning, and after another kiss Eric took his leave. Nell watched at the window as he got into his car and slowly made his way down the drive the girls had shoveled earlier that day. Only when his car was out of sight did she turn to the lighted tree and all the other Christmas decorations with which she had festooned her home. A laugh of sheer joy burst from her. She felt almost dizzy with happiness and the sense of possibility. Why had she wasted so much time assuming only a grim future awaited her when all along she might have been imagining into existence a future filled with pleasure and productivity? *I guess I can toss that newspaper photo of Eric,* she thought, *now that he is mine once again.* But no. She would keep the photo as a reminder of the exact moment her future had begun to open up before her.

Eric had been gone about ten minutes when Nell heard the front door open and shut. It wasn't long before both of her daughters joined her in the kitchen.

Felicity sniffed. "I've seen *It's a Wonderful Life* about a million times, and every single time I cry like crazy at the end."

Molly hefted a large red bag onto the table. "The rest of Mick's gifts," she said with a grin.

"I can't wait to see them!" Felicity cried.

"In a bit," Molly said, looking shrewdly at her mother. "I want to hear about Mom and Eric."

"What makes you think there's something to tell?" Nell asked, barely managing to hide a smile.

"Mom. I read the inscription in the book of poetry Eric gave you."

"What inscription?" Felicity asked.

"Mom will show you later," Molly promised.

Nell took a deep breath. "It's all very simple," she said. "Eric told me that he purposely came to Yorktide to see me. He still loves me, and I still love him. He's going to re-locate so that we can be together."

"OMG!" Felicity cried. "And I said that nothing new or exciting ever happens in Yorktide. I was so wrong!"

Molly took her mother's hand. "I'll admit it was a little disconcerting seeing you with another man today, especially one so obviously in love with you, but it was also a good thing. You deserve to be happy, Mom. And you know what? Remember a few days ago when you asked us what we'd do if we had to create a gingerbread cookie that represented you, and neither of us could come up with anything? We said that you were 'just Mom.' But that's wrong. You're not *just* our mother, you're a person in your own right with your own thoughts and feelings and tal-ents. I'm sorry it took so long for me to understand that."

"I'm sorry, too," Felicity said. "If I had to create a gin-gerbread cookie Nell King I'd make her in the shape of a really big heart."

Nell laughed. "Would I at least have a face?"

"Of course! And you'd have hands and in one of your hands you'd be holding a book of poems and in the other a cookie tin or maybe a glue gun." Felicity turned to her sister. "Okay, now I want to hear about Mick. Did he like the money clip?"

"Yes," Molly said. "And we had a really good talk. We realized that it had been a while since we'd taken the time to talk to each other about the important things in our lives. You were right, Mom. I should have trusted Mick to understand the anxiety I was feeling."

"And?" Felicity prodded.

"And next week we're going to that cool antique place in Portsmouth, Market Square Jewelers, to shop for an engagement ring, something vintage to go with his grandmother's wedding ring. Oh, and the wedding will be next fall, at the farm."

Felicity squealed and threw her arms around her sister. "I had so better be your maid of honor!"

"Of course," Molly assured her.

When Felicity finally let go of her sister, Nell gave Molly a hug of her own.

"I'm so happy for you, Molly," she said. "I really am. So what made Mick come to the house earlier, besides to deliver the fruitcake? It must have taken a lot of courage."

Molly smiled. "He said he had to see me no matter what. When he told his mother where he was going, she said it was about time he claimed the love of his life. And there I was thinking Mrs. Williams must hate me."

"So, what were the other gifts Mick had for you?" Felicity asked. "I'm dying to know."

"An antique milk pail for day eight," Molly said. "I left it by the door for now. Some of them can be pretty dinged up, but this is in really good shape. For day nine, ladies dancing, a Beyonce t-shirt. Then for day ten, lords a-leaping, there was an articulated toy man, the kind with the string you pull to make his arms and legs jump. Day eleven, a CD of Irish pipe music, and for day twelve, a tin soldier with a drum. Totally sweet."

"So, what was the *big* surprise he talked about?" Felicity asked.

Molly grinned. "You're not going to believe this. He bought two tickets to *Hamilton*! That's Broadway! New

York City! And we're going in June, right after graduation, which is a crazy busy time for him, but he said he knows how much I want to see the play and that I mean more to him than even the farm."

Nell smiled. "Now that's saying something!"

"I know! And he's booked us an apartment in Tribeca through Airbnb. It'll be like being a New Yorker for two days. It's very exciting."

"Even though you think people who choose to live in a big noisy city are crazy."

Molly blushed. "Forget everything I've ever said about everything. I'm starting over from this very day. This is a new and better me." Molly shook her head. "I can't believe I was so scared of settling down. I'm *happy* with Mick. I'm *happy* here in Maine. How can happiness be wrong?"

"It *can't* be wrong," Felicity said firmly.

"I agree," Nell said. "Happiness looks like all sorts of things, Molly. You have to choose your own picture of happiness and stick with it."

"You're right, Mom. Hey, do you know what I found out tonight? Mick has always wanted to go to Bora Bora! He never talked about traveling before. I was wrong when I said I knew him thoroughly. There are all sorts of things about Mick I don't know, and I *want* to know them."

"What if *you* don't want to go to Bora Bora?" Felicity asked. "What then?"

"I'll go with him anyway. He's my best friend."

"Loving someone involves compromise," Nell said. "Compromise has gotten a bad rap in the past years. Selfishness has been raised as a goal. But compromise isn't a bad thing in a relationship, as long as you're not the only one doing the compromising."

Molly nodded. "I agree. And I'm going to visit Mrs.

Williams tomorrow and apologize for having hurt her son. Honestly, in spite of her encouraging Mick to fight for me, I'm a bit scared."

"She'll understand," Nell assured Molly. "Why don't you take her a pomander ball? And a few glitter balls. And maybe some cookies. And I'll call her to thank her for the fruitcake."

"You know," Felicity announced, "in some ways this has been the best Christmas ever."

Molly rolled her eyes. "Yeah, in spite of my almost ruining my life by walking away from the best thing that's ever happened to me." She turned to Nell. "Well, the best thing aside from having you as my mother."

The miniature grandfather clock on the mantel of the fireplace in the living room struck midnight. "Another Christmas come and gone," Nell said a bit wistfully.

"There's always next year, Mom," Felicity said, linking her arm through her mother's.

"And the one after that. Hey, maybe when Mick and I get married we could have Christmas Eve dinner at our house for the two families. It could be the start of a new tradition." Molly looked slyly at Nell. "Mom and Eric on one side of the table . . ."

Nell smiled. "That sounds like a great idea."

"And I'll use your great aunt Prudence's platter to serve the roast beef."

"Speaking of food, I'm hungry," Felicity announced.

Molly shook her head in disbelief. "You're a bottomless pit! How can you possibly be hungry after all you ate today?"

Felicity shrugged. "I just am."

Nell went to the fridge and opened the door. "Me too," she said. "How about a cold turkey sandwich?"

"If you insist," Molly said with a laugh. "I'll take mine with cranberry sauce."

Felicity went to the cupboard. "I'll get plates and napkins."

Felicity was right, Nell thought as she began to assemble the sandwiches for her daughters. *This was the best Christmas ever, and it had nothing to do with cakes and crafts and baubles and bells. It had to do with love. Just love.*

OCT 2017